THE HUNGRY GHOST

DALENA STORM

ISBN (print): 978-1-7329357-5-4
ISBN (epub): 978-1-7329357-6-1
ISBN (mobi): 978-1-7329357-7-8

Cover design by Najla Qamber
Edited by Lindy Ryan
Interior design layout by Rebecca Poole

Black Spot Books

This is a work of fiction. All characters and events portrayed in this novel are fictitious and are products of the author's imagination and any resemblance to actual events, or locales or persons, living or dead are entirely coincidental.

For all beings:
Ghosts and ghouls
Dreamers and saints
Witches and fools;
For fish and birds and bees and mice
And gods and demons, flies and lice;
For all who've lived
And all who've died
And all who simply can't decide
What life is for, or why we're born—
May you find shelter from the storm.

CHAPTER ONE

THE HUNGRY GHOST sailed over the land howling as loudly as it could, but the sound that issued out of its tiny, pinhole mouth was little more than a whisper. Spasms racked its bloated and distended stomach. The ghost doubled over, briefly immobilized by the pain. Even moaning hurt its throat. When had it last had something to drink? The ghost couldn't remember. It had been decades, and it longed for something to quench its thirst.

Occasionally the ghost passed what looked like pools of water, but they were only illusions. Even so, the ghost couldn't stop itself from chasing them, hoping that the next one would be different—that the next one would be something from which it could drink—but each time it was the same. The ghost would find a pool it had never seen before; it would rest at the bank and bring its face to the liquid only to watch the water recede before its lips, always just out of reach. The ghost would chase this illusory pool until it was exhausted, and then it would lay, parched and starving, on whatever surface it found itself on—sometimes craggy rocks, sometimes sharp pebbles, sometimes dead dirt from which nothing could ever grow.

There was a reason the ghost was here, but that reason had long been forgotten. Now, there was no room for thought in its existence. Everything was erased by the immediacy of hunger.

Somewhere else, a woman was dying.

Sam did not know she could die.

She knew *other* people could die. Her ex-husband had come close a few times, leaning back in his lawn chair, booze-dazed and heat-dazzled, convulsing in sharp, shuddering seizures she had not believed his soft body capable of. Peter's death had been a constant dark shadow at the edges of Sam's universe; she had dreaded it and anticipated it simultaneously. She had been married to an alcoholic and so that was what she'd done: she'd woken up every morning and asked herself, "Is he going to drink himself to death today?"

Sam had been so caught up in sick fantasies of Peter's death that she never thought about her own. Not in a conscious way, at least.

Mortality hit Sam like that—in a flash of light on the night she might have been the happiest. The rain that fell from the sky was as slick as the oil beneath her tires, and the steering wheel was wrenched from her hands. Her car skittered up the hill, into the left lane. She tried to bear right but the semi came barreling down, its headlights too bright to be real.

It was the noise that hung in Sam's mind the longest, long after the brilliance of the headlights had faded away and everything had stilled. The blare of the semi's horn—

—and then darkness.

CHAPTER TWO

Earlier that night

SAM WAS UNCOMFORTABLE in her dress. The fabric was scratchy and the neckline too wide. It had cost her twelve dollars at the Salvation Army last summer but had mostly resided at the back of her closet since then. She'd only had occasion to wear it once or twice, and even then she'd worn it over layers. Now, it was summer—a hot day, too hot—and she was on her way to meet Madeline even though she knew she shouldn't. Madeline had been one of Sam's student in last year's month-long writing workshop at a university in New York, and she'd had a crush on Sam. At the time Sam had dismissed the girl's crush. It wasn't the first time some pretty young student had lingered at Sam's side, making adoring eyes at her. But it hadn't ended that simply. Right before everyone left to return to their normal lives, the two women had shared a kiss.

It had been a mistake, a momentary lapse of judgment that no one had witnessed. Madeline, however, seemed to have taken it seriously—as some promise of a relationship to come.

Just come and get a drink with me, she'd texted Sam earlier that afternoon. Perhaps it had been the "just"—so innocuous, so innocent, as if the thing she was asking for was not so large as she knew was implied—but the message had hooked Sam in when it really shouldn't have. She was too old for Madeline, thirty-two to her twenty-six. It was only six years, but those six years felt like an eternity. The signs of it were etched across Sam's body. She'd gained weight since that summer, formed wrinkles at the corners of her eyes and the edges of her lips. Madeline would remember her differently, that much was inevitable. She would be repulsed when she saw Sam, but she would try to be polite. Maybe she'd even attempt to sleep with her anyway, but it would be a pity fuck—the worst kind of fuck—and that would only make Sam feel worse.

Sam drafted a response on her phone—*Bad news, ladybug. Something came up.*—but her thumb didn't hit send. She would have to let Madeline down easy. It wasn't that Sam didn't want to see her, it was just that this wouldn't go anywhere—it *couldn't* go anywhere. Sam would fashion a plausible justification. She would ignore the innermost desires of her heart, shutter them away behind thick walls and excuses no one but she would believe. It was better this way. Sam would go back inside and change into something comfortable, maybe get ahead on some grading. She could not enter into a fling of this sort. Not now. Not with everything else she had to do, and certainly not when she was still dealing with the fallout from her ex-husband, who was still drinking and still needing her.

But Sam was already in her car. In fact, she was already

on her way. It was a bit of a drive, enough for most of a David Bowie album, so she deleted the text without sending it and put the phone down in the console. With a deep, steadying breath, she let the music play. When Sam finally found street parking in Harvard Square forty-five minutes later, she maneuvered her car into an open space and killed the engine, hesitating in the silence. She could still leave and avoid embarrassing herself. It wasn't too late.

And then it was.

A sudden knock on the passenger's side window nearly startled Sam out of her skin. It was Madeline's face— fresh, young, trendy—peering in at her, so similar to the photos that had stood in as a representation of her for this past year. Yet, she looked different—more mischievous, more alive. Madeline gestured enthusiastically to Sam, signaling that she should get out of the car. Sam smiled back and resolved to get on with it. She unbuckled her seat belt and slid out of the car, coming around the front to greet Madeline with a hug.

"Hey there, ladybug!" she greeted Madeline, using the nickname she'd called the beautiful younger woman when they'd been in touch.

"I had a feeling that was you when I saw the car coming up," Madeline said. It struck Sam as just the kind of thing that Madeline would say. They hadn't spent much time together last summer, but it had been long enough for Sam to pick up on the fact that Madeline often spoke as if she had access to some hidden level of reality that escaped the notice of everyone else. When she remarked on it Sam almost felt able to believe it, too.

Madeline's voice was teasing and soft. A little hesitant, but familiar. It triggered something in Sam, a feeling she'd tried to push down and stow away for the past year. "How have you been? Tell me everything," Sam demanded as she briefly held Madeline's firm body against hers, then brushed her lips to Madeline's cheek in a friend's kiss, French-style.

"Look at you!" Sam said, drawing back and holding Madeline at arm's length. The truth surprised her when it escaped from her mouth. "It's so good to see you."

"You, too."

Sam could feel Madeline looking at her, analyzing her. Her short hair was in need of a trim; the roots were growing out, the half-inch of brown streaked with gray. Her skin was dry. She wasn't wearing much makeup—only eyeliner, mascara, and lip balm—but she hoped the illusion was holding, that she looked pretty enough.

"It's been too long!" exclaimed Sam.

"I know," Madeline replied, and even though she smiled sweetly there was something in her tone that Sam didn't like. It sounded accusatory, as if Madeline thought it was Sam's fault they hadn't met up sooner.

"What are you doing in Harvard Square?"

"Well, I wanted to see *you* and the only way of doing that seemed to be to make plans to be somewhere and see if you'd show up."

Irritation flared like a fire in Sam. So, Madeline *was* blaming her after all. Lulled into a sense of false optimism by the music on her drive, Sam had thought this reunion might be fun. Now, she wasn't sure it had been a good idea at all.

"Well, you know how it is. I've been busy with the semester. I hardly have time to sleep or eat, so it's been sort of hard to make plans to hang out. Sorry if I've been a bitch."

Sam could feel her mouth curling with bitterness as she tried to distract Madeline with busy talk and self-incrimination. Why couldn't things ever just be pleasant? Why couldn't Madeline just be direct and say *I've missed you!* and give her a big hug? This meeting could have been so nice—an escape from the shit she usually had to deal with—but things never worked out the way Sam wanted. There was always a catch.

"Sam," Madeline said. Her voice was intense and wanting. It made Sam look at her and when she did she couldn't stop looking. "Hi."

"Hi," breathed Sam. Madeline's eyes were so clear. She didn't *look* like she was angry. Sam allowed herself the beginning of a real smile.

"Will you come in and have a drink with me?" Madeline's voice was sweet, almost innocent. The tone of obligation was gone and the question finally felt like an invitation.

Sam laughed, a peal of strange, nervous sound

bubbling up and out of her. It wasn't her usual laugh, but it felt good. "Yes, ladybug. Let's go have a glass of wine. It's been a long week. A long month. Hell, it's been a long year."

"I know," Madeline said, and this time Sam heard the words differently. It wasn't that Madeline had been accusing Sam; this was her way of saying *I missed you*. And she was saying it too, wasn't she? They were both talking around their real feelings—refusing to give voice to them directly—but Sam could hear what Madeline really meant if she listened closely enough.

With that, Sam felt as if all the time that had elapsed between when she and Madeline had last seen each other until now had been bundled into a neat parcel, picked up, and held aloft. They were staring at each other across it, gauging the distance and seeing how it had changed them both, how it had hurt them in different ways, and how even so there were some things that weren't any different at all.

Madeline hadn't been looking for romance when she'd attended the month-long workshop in New York last summer. She'd wanted to learn to write. But from the moment Sam had walked into the classroom and taken her position at the instructor's podium, leaning back against a table and crossing one leg in front of the other, Madeline had been smitten. With her spiky hair and vivid eyes, Sam was the young, punkish, attractive writing teacher Madeline had never known she wanted, and as soon as she saw her, Madeline had wanted Sam more than she'd ever wanted anything. She wanted to touch Sam, to hold her hand, to walk beside her and pass whispered snippets of poetry back and forth. She wanted to follow Sam home to her bedroom, to her bed, where she could wrap her arms around her and learn the rhythms of her body, memorize them by heart.

Sam had remained blissfully unaware of Madeline's attention throughout the duration of the program, but finally, in the end, Madeline had been emboldened by wine and declared what she wanted. "I want to kiss you," she'd told Sam while they had paused on the lawn outside the after-party. Sam was standing there, a freshly lit cigarette dangling in her fingers and half of her face illuminated by the glow from the windows. She froze like that when she was taken by surprise, a picture of startled beauty.

"What?" Sam had asked, hidden in the veil of unfurling cigarette smoke.

Madeline had stepped in and closed the distance between them, and Sam's lips had found hers. The feeling was electric. They embraced in what had surely been one of the most passionate kisses of Madeline's entire life, and Sam's cigarette, forgotten, had dropped and burned itself out on the lawn before they parted.

It had just been one kiss, but it had left Madeline with the burning desire for more.

The next day, Sam left before Madeline had a chance to say goodbye, but they'd exchanged numbers the previous night and so Madeline did her best to keep in touch from her life on the other side of Boston. When Sam wasn't busy teaching, they scheduled phone calls for the weekends and talked about literature and writing, flirtation woven throughout their conversations in a persistent undercurrent of longing. For a while, the calls had been a consistent part of Madeline's weekly routine, but in the last six months the women had lost touch, their calls waning and then stopping altogether. Madeline blamed Sam's husband—*ex*-husband—Peter for driving a wedge between them.

Madeline had wanted to liberate Sam from Peter's grip, and now that he was gone, she wanted Sam for herself. The way Madeline saw it, the timing couldn't be more perfect. She'd texted Sam on a whim, as a last chance opportunity for the two of them to get together, but also—selfishly—because she needed Sam. She needed the inspiration, the adrenaline rush she got when she was with her.

Whenever Madeline wasn't busy working at the coffee shop, she was writing, putting all the things she'd learned from Sam's workshop into practice. Borrowing from mythology, she'd started a new project about a hungry ghost—one that was motivated entirely by its appetite and insatiable desire, much like Madeline's for Sam. It was fiction, of course, but somehow the story had become all tied up with Sam, as things usually did since they'd met. Madeline knew that to overcome her writer's block, something in her situation with Sam needed to move. The stalemate they'd been stuck in for the last year needed to end. So, Madeline had given it a shot in the dark, texting Sam a time and a place even though she hadn't really expected her to reply, much less show up. *Hey lady, I hope you're well! I'm headed to Harvard Square. Give me a call and let me know how you're doing. Or better yet, just come and have a drink with me. Grendel's?*

She'd sent the text and took the subway to the square fully prepared to find some way of entertaining herself on her own. Whenever Madeline had suggested that she and Sam meet up in the past, Sam had responded either just too late or not at all. Luckily, Harvard Square was a place Madeline didn't mind being alone. She could grab a drink at the bar and then wander around the square perusing the novelty shops solo. There was one that carried only Curious George merchandise and a pet store she'd heard about that had a quirky name and was rumored to specialize in unusual cats.

Madeline's text had gone unanswered, but as she'd been making her way down the block toward Grendel's, she'd heard a car approaching. It wasn't as if Sam's car made any particular sound or that Madeline would have recognized it even if it had, but she'd felt in the pit of her stomach: *that's her.* As the car drove past, Madeline saw the figure in the driver's seat had short hair, spiked up in the way Sam had worn it last summer. She'd watched as the driver did a skillful parallel parking job, and when Madeline had trotted up, looking hopefully in through the car window, she had been both surprised and relieved to see it was indeed Sam, here after all, and she was even more beautiful than Madeline remembered.

They were seated at a two-top, separated by two half-empty glasses of wine. The atmosphere was bustling and the conversation had continued at a fast clip. They'd lost track of time.

Madeline had just finished telling Sam how she'd started a new job as a barista that freed up plenty of time for her to write, and how she was as spiritual as ever, involved in a Buddhist meditation group and working on a new story about some kind of ghost.

"It sounds like you're doing really well," Sam told Madeline, then waited for Madeline to return the compliment. Sam never felt like she was doing well, even though she should have. A lot had happened to her in the last year: a promotion, a new class to teach. She was the same as ever in most ways, but better, she hoped. Peter was still in her life. She hadn't been able to change that, even though she had finally—only six months earlier—gone through with the divorce.

And there had been no boyfriends in the meantime, even after the separation was final. "No girlfriends?"

Madeline had asked, and while Sam hadn't liked the implication she'd had to admit that no, there had been no girlfriends either. Madeline had seemed pleased about that.

Sam was still waiting for Madeline to tell her it sounded like she was doing well too, but she didn't. She wasn't going to. Instead, she smiled and was silent, looking at her drink instead of at Sam. Her nails were painted red and she had rubies in her ears. Madeline was self-satisfied, Sam thought. She was used to being adored.

Sam tipped back what was left in her wine glass. This was her signal to leave, to make a quick getaway. They'd already had two glasses of wine each. Sam needed to eat. She needed to grade. Most of all, she needed to escape Madeline.

"Can I get you another?" the waitress asked, appearing out of nowhere.

Sam started to decline, but Madeline interrupted her.

"Just one more?" Madeline pleaded, fixing Sam with her eyes. Sam hid her sigh behind an automatic smile. It was the least she owed Madeline. Probably. One more drink, after a year of avoiding her.

"All right, ladybug," Sam consented, "but this is the last one. I really have to get home."

"I know," Madeline said, and she seemed about to say more, but whatever it was she swallowed it.

The waitress left, and the silence grew in her wake.

"I feel like there's so much I want to say to you," Madeline said, looking at Sam intently.

Then say it, Sam thought, but didn't let the words out. She didn't want to hurt the girl's feelings, but she was frustrated by everything Madeline wouldn't say.

"Or maybe it's not what I want to *say* to you," Madeline continued, more slowly this time, her voice lowering seductively, "but what I want to *do* to you."

At that, Sam's breath caught and she felt herself flushing. Here Madeline went again, being so inappropriate! The girl's arousal, like the time she'd kissed her during the after-party, seemed to come on fast and overbearing—out of fucking nowhere—though Sam couldn't deny that it excited her.

"Is that right?" she asked. She'd meant it to sound coy, but it came out more than a little encouraging.

The waitress arrived with their third glasses of wine. Madeline glanced at her in thanks and then waited for her to leave before taking a drink, as if she was considering what she wanted to say. Sam's heart was pounding. She should shut this down. She shouldn't lead Madeline on. But she could feel Madeline's eyes running over her face and her shoulders, pausing at her chest—not that Madeline's gaze would be rewarded there, considering the baggy fit of this damn dress—but still she looked anyway, perhaps imaging the shape of Sam's breasts under the cloth. Sam could feel her skin reacting, her nipples puckering through her plain cotton bra. What would it feel like, to have Madeline touch her? Would Madeline like her nipples or no? They weren't to everyone's taste.

"I'd like…" Madeline started, and Sam watched her search for the words, her lips parted as if in deep thought. Madeline set her wine down and leaned forward, one of her hands stretching across the table for Sam.

Sam kept her own hands safely out of reach, though the skin on the back of her neck prickled. "Well, I'd start by kissing you," Madeline decided. "Your lips, then your neck." Madeline's eyes continued to trace their way over Sam's body as she spoke, lowering in tandem with her voice, which had grown heavy with want. "Your shoulder. Your arm. The palm of your hand." Madeline reached for Sam's hand, and Sam let her catch it this time, let her bring it to her mouth, where the girl's lips kissed her palm. Madeline's tongue touched her skin and her eyes rolled up to ensnare Sam's. Sam felt an unbidden shiver tremble down her spine as warmth seeped from her belly to between her legs. She pulled her hand back, suddenly shy. "The skin between your breasts," Madeline continued, and there was something very naughty about this sweet young girl speaking as she did, her lips curling lustily.

It made Sam not care that she was older, with graying hair and rough patches of skin. She wanted to take this girl between her legs and hold her there, to ride her nose and the tongue that had brushed her skin. She could imagine Madeline's face covered in her wetness.

She would lick it off. She would eat her up.

CHAPTER THREE

PETER WAS DRUNK again, but who the fuck cared? Sam obviously didn't, or she wouldn't have left. Wasn't a man who'd been kicked out on his ass with nothing but the clothes on his back allowed to blow off some steam by having a little drink? Peter thought so.

He had the very irritating urge to cry yet again and so he swallowed more down from the bottle of Jack Daniels that was lying beside him on the couch. Fuck crying. Peter had to toughen up; he had to be a man. He had to be strong, unaffected, emotionally lobotomized. These were all things he wasn't, which was why Sam had left, wasn't it?

Desperate to avoid his own nagging thoughts, Peter jumped up from the couch and turned on some music. Guns N' Roses. He played it loud, singing along until his lungs ached from the strain of it. His rent was overdue. The landlord would come down in a minute, maybe less, and bang on his door—harass him, the dick—but before he showed up Peter was going to suck up every second he could of this moment of liberation.

Peter pulled his phone from his pocket and took an awkward, fumbling selfie of his gruff, gray-whiskered face. Tattoos showed on his arms, including the one that had been their version of wedding rings. That kind of thing was *permanent*. You couldn't just take it off and *throw it away*. But Sam had thrown it all away, including Peter. She'd thrown him out with the fucking garbage.

Peter thumbed open the social media app. He meant to post the selfie, maybe it would garner a scrap of sympathy—of recognition—but instead he got sucked into the world of Facebook memories. There was their wedding. There was her dress. He remembered her underwear. He remembered the sex. Fuck, he missed the sex.

"I still care about you," Sam had informed him on the day she left, "but I can't pretend that I'm still in love with you. That's not fair to you, and it's not fair to me."

But Sammy, baby, I'll love you forever, was what Peter should have said. Instead, he'd said, "Fine. Whatever. Do what you want" and she had. She'd left him, and made him sign the papers, too. Not that his saying anything different would have changed things. Sam always did what she wanted. It was part of who she was.

Ah, shit. Peter's eyes were watering. It was all over now. It was done!

He collapsed back on the couch and drank more of the whiskey straight from the bottle, enjoying the sensation of darkness overtaking over him, still and black and sweetly quiet. The numbness consumed him and he floated weightlessly in it, but soon the water became a whirlpool. Peter felt his body being sucked down into a drowning darkness, felt his thoughts begin to go blank.

He was going to die without ever seeing Sam again. Of course, she'd remember that the last time they'd talked he'd been a jerk.

Why did he have to be so self-pitying? Why did he have to be so grotesque?

Once, when Sam had still been his wife, she'd touched him with real affection—attraction, even. Yes, he could remember. He'd been skinny back then. He hadn't been so old. He hadn't let the drinking ruin him yet. Peter knew what he looked like now. He was ugly. No, he was *repulsive*—might as well face up to it—and Sam had every right to push him away, to try and find someone else. To be happy without him, since she couldn't be happy with him.

But now, if the drink was killing him—

Peter reached for his phone again and found Sam's name in his contacts. It had been two days since he'd called her. She hadn't returned his last call or the one before it. Peter's heart clenched and it hurt. He doubled over. Was this what a heart attack felt like?

He knew she wouldn't answer, but he tried anyway. The phone rang and rang, until finally the beep instructed him to leave a message. Peter pressed the phone to his ear, imagining Sam on the other end of the line as he babbled incoherently. "Sammy, I'm sorry, but I'm dying. I drank too much. This time I really did it. You don't have to save me, but if you'd just come and see me. I want to see you one last time before I go…"

Peter sobbed into the phone and ended the call, then clutched it to his chest like a lifeline. He was sprawled out on the couch, but it might as well have been a ship afloat at sea. He was completely alone. Sam was the last person who cared what became of him. If she didn't show up, he really would die.

What reason was there left for him to live?

MADELINE COULD FEEL the tide turning as things began, finally, to fall into place. She'd gained confidence; she was no longer tentative, afraid of overstepping a line of authority she shouldn't cross as a student. They were on equal footing this time, and she wasn't letting Sam get away. As Madeline spoke, she saw Sam's face filling with an emotion Madeline recognized: lust. It made Madeline want to tie Sam up, to hold her down, to make her scream.

"Hey," said Sam, and she seemed like she was about to suggest something (*Do you want to get out of here?* Madeline completed in her head) but Sam stopped mid-sentence and, looking annoyed, pulled something out of her bag. She glanced at it beneath the table while Madeline strained to get a look. Sam was looking at her phone.

"What is it? Did someone call?"

"It's nothing," Sam said, but it didn't sound like nothing. It looked like it took serious effort for Sam to force her eyes back to Madeline's and attempt a smile. "I'm just going to run to the restroom, okay? I'll be right back, and then you can finish telling me about everything you want to do to me."

Madeline could tell Sam's smile was meant to be reassuring, so she tried to feel reassured as she sat there, alone again, at the empty table. The waitress stopped by, hesitated, and asked Madeline if they'd have another round, or if they were ready for the check.

"Just the check, I guess," said Madeline, hoping they could take the conversation somewhere more private—Sam's place, preferably, which Madeline had never seen but which she'd heard about and fantasized to be a romantic setting. Sam's address was in Lakeville, Madeline knew, because she'd sent her a Christmas card last year. Sam had been just about to offer to take her there. Madeline was sure she had.

The waitress brought the check and Madeline paid, knowing Sam would have insisted otherwise. Tonight she wanted to take control, and she was sure Sam had said she liked a dominant partner. As Madeline signed the restaurant copy of the receipt, she heard a sudden rush of water on the roof, a deluge from above. The din of the bar muffled the noise, but it sounded like a downpour. Madeline rose from her seat and walked to the entryway, watching the rainfall on the other side of the window. She was still standing there when Sam returned from the bathroom and joined her. Lightning flashed in the distance beyond the city skyline. Thunder crackled and boomed overhead.

It felt like something was coming. A storm, maybe, or something worse.

"It looks like a real summer storm," Madeline mused.

"I love thunderstorms," Sam said, and her voice was such a perfect mix of sad and sensual that it made Madeline grab her hand again. "What are you doing?" Sam asked, protesting, but not very hard, as Madeline pulled her toward the door.

"Come on."

A moment later, they were standing in the rain, getting drenched. Madeline's tank top clung to her skin, and her jeans stuck heavily to her legs. Beside her the flimsiness of Sam's dress seemed to dissolve and Madeline could finally feel her, the *real* her—the warmth of her arms, her ribs, her waist. She pulled Sam into her and for once Sam didn't resist. Her wet kiss pressed soft and hungrily against Madeline's mouth, slippery and sweet.

"I can't," Sam whispered suddenly. She tried to pull away, but Madeline held on.

"Shut up," Madeline hissed, sliding her lips across Sam's cheek to flick her tongue over the wet shell of Sam's ear. Her fingers tangled in Sam's hair, her body going as electric as the sky. Their skin was humming, their heartbeats syncopated, and everything was as it should be. Everything was coming together, everything was so perfect that it took Madeline a minute to process what Sam was whispering between kisses. *"I've got to go."* Why would she say that? Why now? What could possibly—

"I'm sorry, ladybug," Sam said, breaking the kiss. The expression on her face was quite sorry indeed. "I really have to go, but let's do this again soon, okay? Next week, maybe? It was so good to see you."

Next week?

Madeline had lost count of how many times Sam had dangled promises of connection in front of her only to snatch them away. It was part of why Madeline had stopped calling—because of how many times Sam had said to her, "Maybe next week you can come and visit me?" Inevitably something would come up at the very last minute and she'd cancel and it would be up to Madeline to try and reschedule, which never happened. Sam always *seemed* willing. She'd let Madeline get so close she would really believe it was happening...

Madeline wasn't sure she could take that anymore.

"It was good to see you, too," Madeline said. "Why do you have to go?"

Sam was looking at her, holding her at arm's length, beautiful and regretful but immovably firm.

"It's Peter," she explained. "The fucker. He's trying to drink himself to death again. I've got to get him checked into a hospital before he dies, and then it's going to be rehab again... Fuck... I'm so sorry to ruin your night."

"It's okay," said Madeline, not knowing what else to say. It wasn't okay. Sam's excuse made sense, but then again it always did. There had to be a way they could still be together. "Let me come with you."

"No, ladybug. Not tonight."

"Then when?"

Sam ignored her. She had pulled away and was already splashing down the street to her car, going around to the driver's side door, opening it, and getting in. Madeline hurried after her as Sam cranked the engine to life and rolled down the side window, peering back at Madeline from the other side. Just like that, Madeline was once again looking at Sam through a barrier, stuck on the outside of the other woman's life.

Madeline knew she should say something—she should say a million things—but it would have taken too long and there was only a second and then the second was over and Sam was saying, with finality, "Well, bye, ladybug," and Madeline was saying, "Bye" because there was nothing else to say.

Then Sam rolled up her window and drove away as Madeline's life became liquid, spilling away with the rain as it merged with the thousand disparate scattered reflections that shimmered around her in the street.

CHAPTER FOUR

IN ANOTHER PART of Harvard Square, Jimmy had closed up shop for the night, flipping the sign from *open* to *closed*. His store was full of cats still waiting for their forever homes, and he'd just finished feeding the lot of them. Now, he was upstairs in the living quarters above, measuring a piece of lumber he planned to fashion into a cat tree. Jimmy's apartment had a second bedroom that he used as a workshop where he made cat furniture, and he thought he was quite good at it. The patter of the rain on the window soothed away the long day as Jimmy turned on the table saw and passed a piece of lumber through, slicing the wood with a straight cut. Next, he trimmed a piece of base wood to size, a nice big block. Jimmy turned off the saw and began examining leftovers from other projects when a distant and faint meowing cut through the sound of the rain. He paused and listened.

It was the cry of a cat in distress. *Now, who's making a fuss this time?* Jimmy wondered as he ran through the list of usual suspects. There were over two-dozen cats at *Jimmy's Used Cat Emporium*, and he knew them all personally. It could have been Diana, except he'd sent her home with a new family the week before. It could have been Britney or Paul McCartney, and if so, it was probably nothing—just one of them blowing off steam. But the call had a hint of desperation to it and Jimmy couldn't place the voice. Not only that, the sound seemed as though it were located...

He glanced toward the window. The meow was coming from outside the shop.

Jimmy dusted off his hands and went downstairs, where he noticed the rest of the cats were listening to the cry, too. Some of them had gone to sit in the storefront window displays, while others were paused mid-motion, halted in the process of licking, or playing, or sleeping, their ears tipped toward the sound—cautious, curious.

This hadn't happened to Jimmy for quite some time, but occasionally it did happen. A stray would come his way, find itself on his doorstep. Mostly cats didn't venture through this part of the city unless they'd been dumped. Either that or they were adventurous and dumb. No matter which sort of cat this was, it had come this way for a reason, and Jimmy wasted no time as he went through the inner door of the double-entrance, then paused at the front door, opening it carefully so that he didn't startle whoever was out there.

A gray cat, short-furred and young by the looks of her, was huddled in the doorway, soaking wet and shivering. Her tail twitched mightily and when she shifted her position Jimmy saw she was carrying a large belly beneath her.

"By the tail of Macy Gray," Jimmy said, naming her

on the spot. The cat was pregnant, and she looked about to pop.

MADELINE COULDN'T SLEEP. She was lying awake in the darkness, waiting for a text from Sam—an explanation, maybe, or an apology—that never came.

She couldn't stop mulling over the evening's events. She'd been so close, and yet everything had gone just like it had every time with Sam before. Or, rather, it had *not* gone, which was the problem. Madeline had been waiting on Sam for over a year! She'd try to play it cool—she'd stopped calling Sam all the time—but now Sam wanted to put things off until "next week" and Madeline knew that next week would never happen, not if Sam continued prioritizing everything else over Madeline. This was how it always went: Madeline advanced and Sam seemed interested but then she retreated, and somehow it all had to do with Peter. But not just Peter. It was bigger than him, too. What was it that was making she and Sam act the way they did? Where did it come from, and how could she force it to finally change?

Madeline bolted upright in the darkness. She needed to get outside of herself, to see this from another angle. She got up, flicked on the overhead light, and pressed her palms to her eyes as they ached through the adjustment. Blinking and squinting she grabbed her laptop from where it sat on her desk and pulled it with her into bed.

Settling it in on her blanketed thighs, Madeline opened the laptop and then the document of her in-progress story, the one in which a hungry ghost made it into the human world to interfere in the lives of unwitting characters. Even after Sam and Madeline had stopped talking, Madeline had felt their connection. Like the story about the ghost, her almost-romance with Sam was a great, unfinished project that Madeline pulled with her everywhere, and she needed to finish it. She was getting sick of it sitting there, undone. In a way, the aching hunger in Madeline's heart was not unlike that of the ghost's in her story—hungry and greedy, and slowly consuming everything.

Madeline started to write, and she didn't stop until morning.

CHAPTER FIVE

WHILE MADELINE WAS busy writing, Sam's Honda collided with the semi. The horrified truck driver screeched to a slippery stop that blocked both lanes of traffic. Cars honked on either end of him, tires squealing as their drivers slammed on brakes. The traffic jam that followed would last for miles in both directions, but for now, the semi's driver only had eyes for what was left of the tiny car in front of him. Its front was smashed in, crumpled, and the windshield shattered. The trucker's thoughts raced. It wasn't his fault! His brakes couldn't have done anything! He hadn't even had time to try and turn…The rain… Fucking hell, what would his boss say?

The trucker leaped out of his truck and crossed over to the crushed soda can that had once been a compact car. He tried to force open the driver's side door, but it was stuck tight. In the light of the semi's headlights, he could just make out a woman's body in the seat. She was slumped forward and bleeding from the head, her face obscured by shadow and blood. There were no other passengers. The trucker wiped the rain from the window and held his cell phone to his ear under the cover of his baseball hat as he dialed 9-1-1.

Fifteen minutes later paramedics were on the scene.

They retrieved Sam's body and took her away to an intensive care unit in Boston University Hospital where she was then connected to machines that would keep her alive with no guarantee of waking up.

Occasionally, a male nurse passed through, checking on the patients one by one and administering medications as necessary. No one spoke to Sam, and she spoke to no one, but though her body lay there completely non-responsive, her mind was alert and aware.

PETER AWOKE TO the haze of a hangover. His limbs felt heavy and his body ached all over. His mouth was dry. There was a new hollowness within him. Something, it seemed, was missing.

What was it?

Peter rubbed his eyes and looked around. He heaved himself up from the couch and stumbled to the kitchen.

Coffee.

Coffee would fix him all right. No, booze first, and then coffee—or maybe coffee and then booze. Peter could never decide.

Peter dumped grounds into the brew pot, not bothering to use a spoon. He poured water into the machine, switched it on so it started to gurgle, and staggered his way back toward the couch to wait for his head to stop pounding and the world to stop tilting. Where was his phone? What was the news? It was hard to estimate how long he'd been out.

He found his phone wedged between couch cushions, the battery reduced to twelve percent since he'd failed—again—to remember to put it on the charger. Looking at the screen, memories of what he'd done the previous night flooded back to him. He'd called Sam. More than once. *Shit!* What had he said?

"I'm drinking myself to death, you bitch! I hope you're happy!"

Fuck.

His efforts had earned him two voicemails. One of them was from an unknown number, but the other was from her. *Shit.*

Peter's heart pounded, each beat alternating between anticipation and dread. Considering his two options, he pressed play on Sam's voicemail first. Her voice filled his ear. Ohhhh fuck, she was mad. She was ranting. She would kick the shit out of him. She was on her way there. She would be there in an hour—an hour and he'd see Sam!

Peter looked at the time on the message. It'd been midnight when she called. Now it was ten a.m., and she was...where?

He shifted to look out the window. There was no sign of Sam's car on the street outside.

"Sam?" Peter called aloud, but the apartment was quiet. She was obviously not there.

It was unlike Sam to turn around mid-trip. Or, maybe she'd gotten there after all, seen him passed out drunk (again), and said, "*Ah, fuck you*" and left? That was more likely, but still, Peter didn't think Sam would have let him off that easily.

He contemplated the remaining voicemail, which had arrived at two a.m. Could Sam have been calling from a different number? Could something have happened?

Peter didn't want to press play, but it turned out he didn't have to. As he sat there hesitating, his phone began to ring. The same number from the second voicemail flashed across the screen. A chill ran down Peter's spine as he brought the phone to his ear.

"Hello?" His voice was barely a croak. Peter cleared his throat.

"Peter Harrison," a terse voice assumed. "This is Dr. Shah from BU Hospital calling. Your wife was in a car accident this evening."

Your wife. The words echoed in Peter's head, which caused his mouth to hang open. The doctor must have meant Sam, even though she was no longer his wife. She'd made that very clear to him, but she must not have updated her emergency contact information. The slip-up filled Peter with an irrational hope that maybe the divorce had been nothing but a nightmare. Maybe it wasn't too late for him to fix things.

Eventually, Peter managed to say, "What happened? Is Sam okay?"

"She had a collision with another vehicle..." The voice on the other end of the line kept talking, and Peter fought through his hangover to follow along. Sam was in what they called a "non-response state" though her condition was "stable." But what the hell did that mean—Sam wasn't waking up?

SAM'S MOTHER HAD been at the hospital since the emergency room called to deliver the news. When Bianca arrived, she'd been given a plastic bag that contained all of Sam's belongings, all of the things Sam had had on her when she—

No, these things *still* belonged to Sam. Her daughter was alive, and she was going to pull through. Bianca believed this with her whole heart as she clutched the bag of Sam's things tightly against herself.

The password on Sam's phone was the same as it had always been. When Bianca unlocked it she saw all the new messages Sam had received since just last night. Even in the pain of the moment, Bianca swelled with pride. Her daughter was so popular, so loved. She'd been a social butterfly ever since high school. Of course, it wasn't always a blessing. Sam had a way of stretching herself too thin, maintaining relationships that she'd acquired here and there over the years as if she felt some ridiculous responsibility to every Tom, Dick, and Harry she'd ever met. In Bianca's motherly opinion, Sam gave so much of herself—to her students, her friends, even her ex—and got so little back in return.

The most recent message was from a girl, Madeline:

Sorry about last night. Hope everything's okay. Call me?
The name was familiar, but Bianca couldn't place it. She looked at her daughter in the hospital bed and willed her to open her eyes, but Sam's eyes stayed closed.

THE HUNGRY GHOST couldn't get up. Its suffering was too intense. It lacked the strength to push itself to an upright position, and so it lay in the dirt with its face pressed against the ground. Dozens of tiny sharp rocks stabbed into the flesh of its round and distended belly. One jabbed deep into the ghost's cheek, threatening to poke all the way through its skin and into its dry, empty mouth. Long and thin, the ghost's tongue lolled out through its lips. It was far past the point a human being would have starved to death, but the ghost would never die of hunger or thirst. It would continue to exist in this state of starvation until it was released from this life—perhaps in another thousand years, if it was lucky. Too tired and in too much pain to moan, the ghost instead lay silent, its mouth a desert and its belly an empty cave, until it heard a strange sound whispering on the wind. The voice was airy and little more than a gust, but in its wake the ghost heard a distinct word forming—the first it had heard in a very long time, and one it recognized instantly.

Help.

Curiosity rose in the ghost and with it roused a tiny bit of strength, just enough for the ghost to lift its head and look around at its barren environment. The ghost couldn't see very well. Everything appeared as a colorless haze, but the ghost looked as hard as it could and eventually it seemed to see small particles of something in the wind. Perhaps it was dust or leaves... the ghost couldn't be sure, but it could tell they were blowing from a particular direction, which must have been the source of the voice.

The voice was deeply in distress, but no one was listening to it—no one was coming. The ghost knew this with certainty and the knowledge triggered its predatory drive. The thing that was calling was helpless, which meant it would be easy prey. If no one else could hear it, then the ghost could find it. It could take it without contest.

Desire that had fallen dormant in the ghost's belly came roaring back to life as with a great burst of strength it heaved its tiny hands forward and placed them flat on the ground. It began the effortful task of lifting itself upright.

This time, nothing was going to stop the ghost from feeding. This time, it would eat until nothing was left.

CHAPTER SIX

SAM WAS DREAMING, but no matter what she did, she couldn't wake up.

Help! She tried to yell, but her voice caught in her throat. She was tied to the bed, a prisoner in her own body.

This can't be right, Sam thought. *This has to be a dream.* This thought provided a sense of relief, because if it was indeed a dream then she was still in control—if it was a dream, she was not a captive but a creator.

To confirm this, Sam attempted to will things into existence.

Fish, she imagined, and they appeared before her, their scales sparkling like diamonds. She reached for one and it exploded into the multicolored light waves of the aurora borealis. *Birds*, she tried next, and was instantly surrounded by thousands of them—they landed, singing, on her outstretched arms. A small sparrow perched on her right hand and this one used a different voice than the others.

"Oh, Sam, what's happened to you?" the little sparrow said in Sam's mother's voice, and it was shuddering so fearfully that she brought it close to her face, nuzzling it against her cheek as she stroked its head to coax its fear away.

"I'LL HAVE A triple-shot, extra hot, sixteen-ounce vanilla skim latte."

Madeline's first customer of the day greeted her with an order as she attempted to punch all the correct buttons and check the right boxes on the paper cup.

It was a struggle, but eventually Madeline fell into the hypnotic rhythm of the day. Even her emotions assumed a reliable pattern, cycling through worry, fear, hope, and frustration and back again. It had been a late night, but she'd made it through the first draft of her story and it was coming along pretty well so far. It was about a ghost trying to find its way out of suffering, but it was more than that. It was also about Sam and herself and what kept happening between them, though the ending still wasn't coming out right. Too many obstacles kept getting in their way, screwing up the storyline. Madeline was sure that if she could just tell the right story, then maybe she could change things in her real life, too.

She could finally change her life—and Sam's.

Madeline finally got a chance to check her phone when she went on break at ten-fifteen. She saw—at last!—that Sam had texted her back.

But no, something was wrong. The words on the screen weren't Sam's after all.

This is Bianca, the message read, *Sam's mother. I just wanted to let all of Sam's recent contacts know she's been in a car accident and is currently at BU hospital, Room 409. She is stable, but the doctors are not yet sure which way things are going to go. Visiting hours are between ten and four, and well wishes are welcome, but please don't call or text this number right now. If you need to contact me directly, my number is...*

Madeline read the text once, and then again, and then a third and fourth time. Her thoughts were scrambled and she was at a complete loss for how to react. The doctors weren't sure which way things would go? A car accident? When? Not last night... Madeline remembered the rain and how distracted Sam had been when she'd left Grendel's. Madeline had tried to stop her, but maybe she'd given up too easily. Was this partly her fault?

THE DOCTORS HAD just finished taking Sam's vitals when Peter walked in, and Bianca was too focused on her daughter to fully conceal her negative reaction. She tried to paint over it with a smile, but it felt thin and forced. Why the hell had they let him in? He was Sam's *ex*-husband; he had no business being here.

"Hi, Bianca. I came as fast as I could."

"Peter." The smile still hadn't reached Bianca's voice by the time she greeted Peter. "Shouldn't you be at work?"

His eye twitched. He averted his gaze. His posture was hunched, his belly round from drinking.

"Uh, well, you see..." His words floundered and then faded.

Bianca knew it. Peter was unemployed. Again.

"The doctors say her condition is stable," Bianca spoke just to fill the silence, sparing Peter the humiliation of having to explain himself further. "Sam might wake up at any moment, or she might not wake up at all. If her unresponsiveness continues for forty-eight hours, she will officially be in a coma."

Bianca had grappled with the gravity of this statement all morning, and now that she said it she took some perverse pleasure in seeing horror fill Peter's face. It served him right for always clinging to Sam like a lifeline—always putting the responsibility on her to fix things for him. Bianca wondered what he would he do now that Sam wasn't around to save him. Maybe he'd have to actually face the consequences of his actions.

BEFORE HER BREAK was officially over, Madeline returned to the café to seek out its owner. She found Christina ducked down behind the counter, replenishing the supply of paper cups. As Madeline reached her, Christina stood up sharply, so that the two nearly collided.

Christina took one look at Madeline's expression and saw that something was wrong. "Do you need something?"

Madeline was still holding her phone, and she held it up as if in explanation. "I have a family emergency. I need to go to the hospital."

Christina furrowed her eyebrows, glanced at the phone in Madeline's hand, and sighed. A long line of customers was waiting impatiently at the counter, and there was only one other cashier at the register. "We're a little short-staffed right now—"

"It's urgent."

Christina glanced back at Madeline and gave in. "All right, fine. You can go ahead and get out early, but will you be available later this evening?"

"I don't know," said Madeline, already walking away.

"Well, call me when you know! We could really use someone at—"

The door had already closed behind Madeline before Christina could finish.

CHAPTER SEVEN

WHEN MADELINE ARRIVED at the hospital, she made her way slowly down a long narrow white hall, each step filling her with a sense of growing dread. Would all of Sam's family be there? Would Madeline have to make small talk? Would they have any idea who she was? Sam had mentioned Madeline to her mom, hadn't she? Once or twice, at least? She hoped she wouldn't see anyone. She only wanted to see Sam, to tell her she was sorry—that she shouldn't have let Sam go, or at the very least she should have gone with her. She should be lying next to her in that hospital room. She wanted to shake Sam, and kiss her, and hold her, and wake her up.

Madeline stopped at Room 409. This was it. Madeline hesitated as she looked through the small window on the door at the crowd gathered inside. As she watched, a fit, youngish man with brown hair turned away from the group and began moving in her direction. Quickly, Madeline pushed the door open and stepped inside, holding the door open for him.

"Hello." He greeted her without recognition in a voice thick with emotion as he slipped past. Sam had mentioned she had a brother. Perhaps that was him.

Around the corner, Madeline saw a man whose face

she did know. Peter. She recognized him at once from her late-night stalking of Sam on Facebook. He was standing near Sam's head, just behind her mother, Bianca, and he looked as much of an outsider there as Madeline felt.

"Peter?" asked Madeline, and Peter turned to look at her, surprised.

"Do I know you?"

Of course he didn't—not by sight anyway—but maybe Sam had told him about her. "My name is Madeline. I was one of Sam's students at a writing retreat last year."

Madeline was pleased to see recognition dawn in Peter's eyes, followed quickly by jealousy as he sized her up. "I see," he said, his eyes narrowing. "That's right. What are you doing here?"

"Last night…" Madeline's words trailed off as members of Sam's family turned in her direction. She waited for them to resume their conversations before continuing on more quietly, moving closer to Sam's ex-husband. "I was with Sam last night. We got together for drinks, but she left early because, well, she said she got a call from *you.*"

Peter's jaw stiffened and he looked away, avoiding Madeline's gaze. She watched a flush creep up his cheeks. "They brought her in last night around 11 p.m.," he said in a conspiratorial voice too low for the others to hear. His breath smelled like stale liquor. "She's been unconscious ever since. Apparently, if this goes on for forty-eight hours, they'll officially call it a coma, but that's just a technical term—she could still wake up at any time. So, in the meantime, they said it's good to talk to her…"

Though she wasn't sure why, Madeline realized she was avoiding looking at Sam directly. She made herself look, and something about the scene made her recoil, shivering.

"Cold?" asked Peter, smirking.

"A little, maybe. Yeah."

Peter shrugged. "They keep it chilly in here."

Something was swelling inside of Madeline and it was very hard to remain still. She felt like she was supposed to stay, but all she wanted was to get out of there. "Well, I guess I should be going," she mumbled at last, awkwardly. She should make some kind of gesture, some show of support. Sam's left foot was sticking up under the sheets and Madeline grabbed it, giving it a gentle squeeze as she tried not to shudder at the cold, deathlike hardness of Sam's skin.

As HE LEFT the hospital Peter wondered if Sam would ever pick a woman over him. They'd discussed it before. She'd thought she was a lesbian once, back in college, but had ultimately decided against it. Did desires like that return? Had she outgrown it but now gone back—or perhaps it had been there all along, buried within her while they were married.

"I don't love genders. I love people," Sam had been

fond of saying, which had not really been an answer either way.

And anyway, wasn't it different? Didn't it have to be? A cock was not a vagina; a vagina was not a cock. Those were the facts, and no one could say otherwise. So given the choice, which would Sam prefer?

Of course, it wasn't that simple, Peter knew. It was *his* particular cock versus *Madeline's* particular vagina. Young, pretty little Madeline against fat, old, crotchety tattooed Peter. An image emerged in his head: a cartoon of the two of them depicted as walking genitalia, wearing nametags and standing on either side of Sam's hospital bed.

Well, that was sick. No wonder Sam didn't like him.

No, it wouldn't do to think like that.

Sam had nearly died. That reality was forcing Peter to see his life in a new light. Now, he could see that anything was possible—and that he didn't have endless time. Today was the day he would give up drinking. No more relapsing, no more rehab. He would go cold turkey and do it on his own, and if he ever slipped up again he'd say goodbye cruel world for real.

It was time for Peter to get his shit together. On the six-block walk to the subway, a sign on the window of a bakery caught his eye.

HELP WANTED: BAKERS

It was a sign, the glimmer of opportunity Peter had been waiting for. He had twelve years' experience in customer service, and a good seven of these had been spent in food service. He'd worked as a cook and a line chef at high-end restaurants; he could certainly bake a loaf of bread. He even had his own recipe for rye. He'd worked it out a few years back. Sam had liked that one, and she'd always been picky about bread. She'd made sandwiches of Peter's rye without leaving hardly anything for him. It was a perfect opportunity. He'd pop in and fill out an application, and by tomorrow, he'd be employed! His life would come together. Sam might even come back to him. By the time she woke up, he'd be a different man—the one she'd loved once upon a time.

The smell of freshly baked bread hit Peter as he pushed open the door to Breadwinner Bakery and made his way to the counter to request an application. There was flour in the air and the smell of yeast was nostalgic. Peter remembered when he and Sam had shared a home. Things had been so nice then. Peter would cook and Sam would grade and they'd go to bed not afraid to touch each other. Those were the days. That had been bliss. He saw that now. And it wasn't too late; it didn't have to be over.

CHAPTER EIGHT

TIME PASSED DIFFERENTLY while Sam was locked inside her head. For the first few days, she was flooded with dream after dream, each rising up like a wave and crashing through her mind in disarray, scattering sensations, emotions, images, and thoughts. She floated from one dream to the next without recalling the last, each new dream immersing her in its world as it tumbled her about, until it eventually left her on the beach of her mind and the next arose.

Though her mind moved through the dreams, Sam could not toss and turn in her bed. Her body began to ache from the strain of staying still. She started to dream of confinement, of straight jackets, of torture, and of things even worse. She felt the incredible need to move, but no matter how she tried she stayed still. Immovable. She re-lieved herself where she lay, which forced her to dream of defilement and anger and revolt and disgust. She dreamed of sex. She met past lovers. She sucked them off, was eat-en out. She became them for a while, and then people she didn't know. She managed to escape from herself, and in so doing brushed through other possible lives—at one point a young boy, then a grown man, a fat woman, and a bluebird. Eventually, she was Sam again, but not Sam as she was now. Sam of different times, of six years old and of ten. Sam of thirty, going on a hundred.

In real time, a week passed, and visitors came frequently, whispering into her dreams.

I love you, my baby girl.

I need you, Sammy. Please wake up.

You can beat this thing, Sam. You're the strongest woman I know.

Sam could hear them, and in her dream world apparitions emerged, shadows of the people who owned each of the voices. She dreamed of her mom baking a pie, of her brother taking her on a boat. She dreamed of Peter when they'd first been married, only in that dream he looked as he did now and where she should have felt lust and love she felt the hot shame of disgust instead. She dreamed of Madeline and the way they had kissed in the rain.

After a while, Sam's brain began to adapt to a new rhythm. Amidst the constant waves of her dreams, she felt her head emerge at last above the water.

Sam opened her eyes and looked around. She was in an empty room, surrounded by flowers. It must have been night, but despite the darkness she was able to see clearly, and when she sat up and looked behind her she was able to recognize that it was her own face she saw lying in bed, eyes closed. It struck her that she looked broken and pale, and not much like the image of herself she had last seen in the bathroom mirror on the night she had readied to meet Madeline—a night which now seemed a lifetime ago. Breathing tubes were stuffed up her nostrils. An IV drip was taped to her arm.

The body lying in the bed was Sam's, but simultaneously not hers at all. If she was sitting here, looking at herself, then how was the body in the bed still breathing? How was any of this possible?

Gripped with a sudden terror of death, Sam lay back down in the bed and closed her eyes, crossing her arms atop her for comfort as she willed the nightmare to end. *Please wake up, please wake up, please wake up*, she begged herself, but rather than waking up, Sam only managed to lull herself right back into the realm of her dreams.

CHAPTER NINE

BIANCA, WHO HAD never been to medical school but who knew how to use Google, needed to teach these doctors a thing or two about medicine—or more specifically, about bedside manner. They should be calling Sam by her name every time they saw her, not ignoring her, and they really should consider giving her a dose of Zolpidem, a sleeping aid that was known—paradoxically—to sometimes help awaken patients from comas. That was what they were calling it now, a coma, seeing as how it had been two weeks since the accident. The term seemed somehow pejorative to Bianca, and she wished the doctors wouldn't use it in Sam's presence. Still, no matter how nicely she phrased her suggestions, they reacted the same as the fourth graders she'd taught every day for thirty years—which was to say they made a lot of grunting sounds or silently disagreed while avoiding her eyes.

Nothing if not a patient woman, Bianca was doing what she could to help Sam. She had brought all of Sam's favorite books—*Charlotte's Web*, *Anne of Green Gables*—and had been reading them to her. Sam was a literary thinker. Not *literal*, but *literary*. Stories were her life's blood. They spoke to her soul.

Through the coma, Bianca was convinced, they could speak to Sam, too.

There was a bookmark in *Charlotte's Web*, a slip of paper stuck a little over halfway through. Bianca opened to the page, wondering who had been reading it last.

"Do you understand how there could be any writing in a spider's web?"

"Oh, no," said Dr. Dorian. "I don't understand it. But for that matter, I don't understand how a spider learned to spin a web in the first place. When the words appeared, everyone said they were a miracle. But nobody pointed out that the web itself is a miracle."

Bianca smiled, imagining her daughter reading the passage to one of her granddaughters, probably Rosa, and sighed. She looked at Sam and her heart trembled. It was hard to hang on to the ledge of grief like this, unable to let go but aching from the effort of holding on. She wanted her daughter to wake up. She did. But she also wanted what was best for Sam, and what was that? Could this really be what was best for her? She was spending every day attached to machines while her ex-husband leered over her like some kind of leech subsisting on her blood. Bianca feared this was destined to become another situation turned selfish: Sam trying to get away, and all of them holding tight, desperate to keep her where she was—no matter the cost.

All Bianca had ever wanted was for Sam to be happy.

She'd have given anything to give her daughter that. It was the one thing she'd failed at as Sam's mother.

THE NEXT TIME Sam was aware of herself, the sun was shining on a beautiful day on the world outside her window. She recognized the walls of the hospital room around her, but this time didn't look at the figure in the bed. Instead, she turned her attention to the window, wondering if she could go outside.

Sam had hardly thought it before she found that she had passed through the glass of the windowpane. Not only that, but she was hovering in the air six floors above the ground. A dizzying sense of vertigo came and then dissipated, and Sam felt free in its wake. This was the first time in many years she had felt entirely and completely free.

Her vision was different. She was able to see three hundred and sixty degrees around herself, and she explored the world around her, twisting her line of sight as she did. She could see through things, too. Not in the form of images—not exactly—but rather a sense of the solidity of things that existed behind walls. Euphoria flooded her, and Sam recognized the sensation from her childhood. It permeated her like sunlight and lit up her soul. Had it really been that long since she was truly, completely happy?

Where should she go? What should she do? The world was waiting, and Sam could fly.

Sam lifted herself higher, above the hospital, and then higher still so she had a view of the city. A hawk glided lazily past her, catching the current and letting itself be carried on the wind. Its predatory eye flashed keenly, white showing around the pupil, but it couldn't see Sam, and so it passed on, scanning for prey.

Arriving at a low-hanging cloud, Sam paused and surveyed Boston below. Her house was outside the city, down the highway, resting in a small town by the lake. She could go there and sit on her porch and listen to the birds as they came by the feeder. She could go instead to her mother's house, north of the city, and see what she was up to. Or, she could stay right here and meld with the sunlight. She could let her ties to everything drift away. She could rest for a while, away from it all.

Sam floated in place and the world moved at its own pace around her. Clouds drifted past, some high, others low. Ducks and geese, crows and hawks flew past. All of the various things that had pulled Sam this way and that before couldn't reach her up here. She felt guilt, followed by giddiness. This was wrong, but it felt so good. She was ignoring all of her responsibilities. No one knew where to find her.

CHAPTER TEN

IN THE SPHERE of Madeline's story, there were six realms of existence, each defined by Tibetan Buddhists. Residing in the uppermost realm, with the most comfortable and powerful lives, were the gods. Below them lived the demigods, and below them, the humans. Rebirth as a human, though not the highest possible birth, was of all births the most auspicious, for only a human could attain enlightenment. In the lower realms were the animals, and below them, the hungry ghosts. Lowest of all were the hell beings.

In the weeks that Sam slept, Madeline continued to write, her story taking shape as it moved beyond her desire, dipping into the barren, alternate universe of the hungry ghost. Starved of inspiration, Madeline's mind became focused on a single hungry ghost, one who had been consumed with longing for so many eons it had forgotten who it was—or who it once had been—but who had been presented with the opportunity to escape from the realm that held it prisoner. Greed had consumed it to the point that hunger defined it; it was no longer an individual with a name and a past but an empty, aching vessel. It had gone so long without eating that its hunger had become insatiable, and now, even if it were presented with the opportunity to feed, nothing would be able to satisfy it.

As Madeline wrote, she ached with a burgeoning longing, imagining Sam in the rain and Sam driving away. She, too, wanted what was impossible.

Madeline, like the ghost, was hungry.

THE HUNGRY GHOST had been following the voice on the wind for a very long time. For hungry ghosts, time passed differently, and so it might have been a week or it might have been a year since it had first heard that faint, pained cry. Seizures twisted its stomach every few seconds and between them, a dull, empty ache lingered in the hollow part of what might have been its heart. Still, it couldn't stop moving, because whenever the ghost stopped to catch its breath the voice on the wind taunted it, jabbering on inanely about fish and birds and spiders and webs, filling the ghost's head with fantasies of bloated arachnids. It would gobble them up webs and all.

Over time, the voice grew louder until it seemed to be coming directly from the sky overhead. The ghost stopped, looking up at the empty sky, but it could see nothing. The voice was saying something about someone named "mother" and using the word "love" over and over again, and then, all at once, it stopped.

The voice had gone quiet before for periods of time, but always a faint murmur continued in the background. Sometimes it sounded like little more than rhythmic breathing.

This silence was different. It was complete and total. A sudden rage filled the ghost. If ever the ghost discovered who or what the voice had belonged to, it would make that thing suffer for being the source of this awful hope. To make it believe relief was coming only to have it snatched away at the last second. The ghost's body shook with a combination of rage and desperation, but when it turned its eyes upward again it saw the sky had developed a strange quality. It was almost like there was a tunnel in the gray, a place where the air itself seemed absent and some force was pulling it toward the source of a very distant light.

The ghost's black eyes widened. Was this a way to escape?

There was a glint of movement very far overhead, and the ghost sensed it needed to act quickly. It dove upward toward the light, following it through the rift between the planes as it aimed for its distant source. The ghost felt like it was being squeezed very tight, very tiny, very small, and then, at last, it saw the opening to a different, higher plane. Up there, it realized, was the promise of much greater delicacies, of rich sauces and fine wines and sensual pleasures galore. It saw tables set with plates and cutlery and all-you-can-eat buffets. It saw piles of fruits and vegetables and buckets of salty, fried animal legs—none of them running, none of them still attached, all of them just sitting there, waiting to be eaten. In the urgency of its struggle, its hunger pains nearly vanished, and then it was through—

All was spacious. All was still. All was calm.

The ghost found itself in a small, cold room. On a bed beneath it was a vacant shell, sprawled out and empty. It had four appendages and a large face; its skin was pale and tubes were stuffed up its nose. The hair on top of its head was short and two-colored: brown at the skull and yellow at the tips. The ghost did not know gender and could not tell the difference between one of these creatures and another, but this must have been the thing that was speaking—the source of the voice. From the deep recesses of its memory a word rose to its mind—*human*—and along with the word came the certainty that this human body was currently unoccupied. Whoever had been inside had stepped out, abandoned this shell, and the ghost found itself fixating on the marvelous size of the human's mouth.

The things it could eat with such a mouth!

The ghost dove into the empty body that had once belonged to Sam, and there it stretched out, trying to figure out how to make its new body respond.

WITH A BLUSTER of wings, a crow flew through Sam and then cocked its eye back at her as if to say, *What are you doing?*

Sam was pleased the crow could see her as everything else she had seen so far had ignored her. "Do you want me to follow you?" she asked, and though the crow didn't reply, Sam followed it anyway. She could sense it had a destination from the purposeful way it cut a straight line through the air over the city before descending into a neighborhood on the edge of Harvard Square, not far from the bar where she'd met Madeline in a time she only barely remembered now. Sam rode on the crow's tail feathers as it swooped down to street level. The trees grew up around them, and the crow landed on the sidewalk before hopping into the gutter where it pecked at a bit of sesame bagel. Sam watched it for a while but the bird had forgotten her, and so she turned her attention to the street full of pedestrians. They walked past and through her hurriedly while talking on cell phones or listening to music. Moving on, Sam slipped through the door of the nearest building and was surprised to find the room filled with cats.

They were everywhere, prowling around the carpeted floor and lounging on tall wooden cat trees and shelves. They sharpened their claws on cardboard scratching posts and ate from bowls of dry cat food. Some were sleeping on the windowsill, where bright sunlight filtered in to heat the room. Emblazoned on the window, in reverse, Sam could read the name of the shop: *Jimmy's Used Cat Emporium.*

The only human in the place was a strongly built black man, who she guessed must be Jimmy. His hair was cropped closely at the sides and short and curly on top, and he was wearing a fitted white tee shirt that exposed the muscles of his forearms. Jeans hung loosely on his hips. He was sitting on his heels on the floor, bending over a little gray cat with a large, swollen stomach.

Sam drew in closer, examining the man's face. He had smooth, supple skin and smile lines that creased his eyes, but he'd lived a life of worry, too, Sam felt, studying him. He was older than her by a good twenty years or so, but he handled the cat in front of him with a gentleness that made Sam ache. How she longed for someone to touch her like that. The cat—pregnant, Sam realized—panted and whined.

"There, there," said the man. "It won't be much longer."

Sam was still adjusting to her new vision, and it took her a while to figure out that the five pulsing lights she saw in the belly of the cat reflected each of the lives waiting within her stomach—one for each of the five kittens she carried. Four of the lights were bright and white, but the fifth was weaker, mawkish, and blue. That one was buried deepest in the cat's belly. Sam had a flash of understanding: she was seeing life before it was born, and one of those lives was in danger. The final kitten in the cat's belly was the runt, and its fate had already been sealed.

Unless Sam did something, it was going to die.

Drawing close, Sam peered into Jimmy's kind brown eyes as she filled the space between the man and the cat. As he stared at the expectant mother, Sam suddenly—*desperately*—wanted his eyes to see her. No one had ever looked at her that way, with pure love. It wasn't the need that lurked in Peter's eyes or the desire in Madeline's. It was different, too, than what Sam saw in her own mother's eyes, a sort of protective passion that was as demanding as it was giving.

Acting on instinct Sam dove for the cat's belly, sliding through its fur as she entered its womb. Once there, Sam focused her attention on the faint blue light that pulsed feebly from the dying kitten. She pushed, trying to enter the kitten through its belly, just as she'd entered the mother cat, and the blue light yielded, dislodged easily by her forced entry. Sam expanded inside the kitten's small, soft body, her own light growing brighter and stronger as it eclipsed what remained of the weak blue glow.

This space was Sam's now, and she was wrapped in warm darkness. She could hear a strange sound, loud and overpowering. *Thu-thump, thu-thump.* It was quick and rhythmic, and it drowned out Sam's thoughts with its hypnotic repetition as it grew louder and more insistent. She had a brief flash of terror: what was she doing? Where was she? Could she get back out if she wanted to, or was it already too late?

Thu-thump, thu-thump, banged the mother cat's heart, and a keen whining sound came from an outer chamber.

A massive earthquake shook the world around her, and Sam felt the bodies of the other four kittens slither and slip around her. Sam gave herself over to gravity and momentum as she was pushed outward headfirst. She was being born again.

IN ANOTHER ROOM, far away, the ghost had stretched to fill the empty shell it had found in the bed. Things sutured into place as it solidified itself into its host's limbs and bones. No longer a wandering spirit, the ghost now had a ribcage, a stomach, two meaty legs, two dangly arms. Wrists, shoulders, a neck, a head, a jaw. Teeth.

It breathed through its nose. Sound came through its ears. The air tickled its skin.

It was hungry.

The ghost opened its eyes.

CHAPTER ELEVEN

DELIVERING KITTENS WAS one of Jimmy's special pleasures. He'd never lost a mama cat, though often a few of the litter wouldn't make it. It was terribly exciting to see what color the little furballs would turn out to be, how many were boys and how many were girls.

Macy Gray did all the work. Five healthy kittens slid from her womb as Jimmy sat back with a towel, letting her lick them clean as he watched carefully for telltale signs that she'd attempt to gobble any. He kept the other curious cats a safe distance away.

A change came over Macy as she pushed out the final kitten. A deep, guttural growl rose from her throat and her claws slipped through the fur of her paws. Instinctively, Jimmy's scooped up the kitten, swaddling it protectively in the towel. He received just one little scratch on the back of his right hand from Macy Gray as he soothed the shivering kitten's body. Eyes closed, its body damp, the kitten seemed only half alive, as if it hadn't made up its mind whether to stay in this world or not.

"There, there," Jimmy cooed, wrapping the kitten so that only its tiny face peeked out. Jimmy knew what it was like to be rejected by a mother; he'd never even met his own. The kitten's mouth hung open in a silent mewl, begging for food but seemingly too startled to speak. "It'll be formula for you, little...lady," Jimmy said, checking. "And for a name, it must be... Mickey. After Michael, the youngest of the Jackson Five. He was at his best, back then. Just a fresh young kid. I sure wish he could've turned into the man I knew he could've been."

THE GHOST'S NEW body was uncooperative. It was sluggish and weak. Hunger raged in its stomach but it wasn't able to move to satisfy it. The ghost wanted to howl in frustration, but the most it could manage was a low moan. When it would moan, people would rush to it, pet its head, and give it an injection that forced it into a state of hazy consciousness. Even sedated, the ghost would never actually sleep, which made its agony worse. It was awake in the new body that had called out to it, but the ghost couldn't control it. It could do nothing to quell the pain of hunger.

On the first morning, the ghost ignored the humans who came and harassed it. One human held a small device close to the ghost's head, and strange, hypnotic, and repetitive sounds came out of it. The human then said, "Remember when we danced to that, Sammy?" and sat, staring at the ghost, waiting for some sort of response it didn't give. Other humans insisted on talking and talking as if the ghost wanted to listen, but it did not want to listen—it wanted to get up.

It wanted to eat.

As the ghost lay inert, striving for motion, it became aware of the needs and demands of its body. Different desires peaked and quelled, depending on the time of day and the sort of injections it received. Some of its urges were not consumptive but eliminative, and those would happen in abrupt bursts, after which it would be soiled until another human came to clean it off again.

This banal human life, the ghost quickly learned, was nothing more than a new kind of hell. Where were the buffets, the animal legs? The rich sauces and fine wines it had imagined? Why had it escaped the realm of hungry ghosts if things were hardly any better here?

Nevertheless, the ghost was forced to observe the humans around it. They came in different sizes and were distinguishable by face shapes and names. One particular human face rose out of the background when it leaned over and took the ghost's hand. This human was there more often than all the others, always with the useless talking.

"We'll have a big party, darling, as soon as you're well, with all your favorite foods. I'll get Carly to make Coq au Vin, authentic French style, and I'll make pie. We're all rooting for you, my strong girl. I love you to the moon and back."

The ghost vainly attempted to focus on this all-important face and tried to distinguish its features from those of the other humans. Its eyes were big and brown, its hair dark and short, curling down to a pointed chin. It had small lines coming off the corners of its eyes and on either side of its mouth, which was redder than most mouths and always turned upward at the corners. The eyes hardly ever blinked. The human also had a soft, protruding chest, which not all humans seemed to have. The ghost felt an odd fondness for this chest, as if it were somehow important to it. The human's name was Bianca, and it seemed to think the ghost's name was "my girl" or maybe it was "love."

ONCE SAM AWOKE, the early weeks of her recovery passed quickly for Peter. He had used her hospitalization as a wake-up call, a signal to get his life into gear before she came back to her senses, and he'd thought he was making excellent progress. His calendar now showed forty-seven checkmarks in a row, one for each day he hadn't had a drink. This was a technique he'd acquired in one of his stints in rehab: visual reinforcement for meeting goals. It sounded sappy, but it worked. Seeing those marks made Peter feel like he'd accomplished something—like he was headed for something good.

But it wasn't enough. At the rate Sam was recovering she'd be walking and talking in no time, and Peter still didn't have a job. The bakery hadn't called him back, and last month's rent was overdue. "You just have to try harder," is what Sam was going to tell him, just like she always had before. But damn it, he was trying! It was the world that was against him. He didn't even look employable. Had she taken a look at him lately?

But no, of course she hadn't. Her eyes were open but she hadn't recognized him yet at all, he reminded himself.

He almost smiled but stopped. There was nothing about Sam's condition to smile about, but it did mean she wasn't actively being mad at him. Maybe with a little luck, by the time Sam was back to herself he'd be different. He was getting clean, and this time…this time he'd stay that way.

The theme to *The Fast and the Furious* started playing on Peter's phone and he nearly dropped his coffee mug in his scramble to answer it.

"Hello? This is Peter Harrison." His voice sounded eager and excitable, even to him.

"Hey, yeah, Peter, this is Tony from Breadwinner Bakery. I'm calling to see if you were still interested in the job."

Peter grinned. It looked like lady luck was on his side after all.

CHAPTER TWELVE

PETER'S INTERVIEW WAS scheduled for ten-thirty the next morning. Resume in hand, he pushed open the door to Breadwinner Bakery at exactly ten twenty-nine. There was a short line at the counter. Shit, the fucking subway had screwed him. Could he go to the front, or was he going to have to wait? After a brief moment of hesitation, Peter headed straight to the counter, trying to catch the eye of the young female cashier. "Hello," he tried, but either she didn't hear him or was ignoring him as people in line started to turn and look and glare. The door to the store opened and a young woman with a double stroller came partway through the doorway and then appeared to get stuck. Feeling chivalrous, Peter abandoned the counter and dashed for the door, holding it back as the woman struggled to maneuver her way in.

He'd been the hero, but now it was ten-thirty and he didn't see any choice but to wait in line. When Peter finally reached the counter, it was ten-thirty-four.

"What can I get for you?" the woman asked.

"I'm here for an interview."

"Sorry? I didn't get that."

Peter held up his resume, showing her that this was official business; he didn't want a muffin. "I'm here for an interview with…" the owner's name suddenly slipped his mind. "An interview. For the bake shop."

"With Tony? Is he expecting you?"

"Yes. I'm his ten-thirty."

She glanced up at the clock on the wall and rolled her eyes. He was late. She was seeing that he was late—that he was five fucking minutes late, no thanks to her selective hearing. *So professional*, Peter scolded himself.

"Go on around back," she said, gesturing with her head to a door behind her in a movement that concurrently dismissed him and motioned the next customer forward.

Peter maneuvered himself around the counter and made his way through to the back. The guy's name was Tony. Tony. Tony. *Tony.*

He wandered past a restroom and was presented with a choice of three more doors. Peter paused, feeling himself briefly in some kind of game show—*And behind door number three, Johnny*—he tried to peer through the blurred glass windows, but all was foggy. When he reached the end of the hall the last door opened and a man walked out—almost right smack into him.

"Oh," said the man, blinking, startled.

"Are you Tony?" Peter asked. "I'm here for an interview. My name's Peter Harrison. Sorry I'm late."

"Ah, yes. Fine. Nice to meet you." The man who must have been Tony extended his hand and shook Peter's firmly. Peter's own handshake was wimping out, getting crushed. He redoubled his efforts and grasped harder.

"You, too," Peter said, affecting a deeper voice as he met Tony's eyes. He gave Tony's hand an extra hard squeeze before releasing it.

"Go on in," said Tony, shaking Peter's grip out of his hand. Peter winced. Maybe he'd squeezed too hard. It probably wasn't a good thing to crush the boss's hand. "Have a seat. I'll be with you in a minute."

"Certainly."

The minutes that passed while Peter sat in the office prepping for the interview seemed to him, in retrospect, to have lasted longer than the interview itself. He had so many possible stories he could have relayed, so many funny and relevant anecdotes he could have offered, but Tony simply glanced over his resume and noted the gaps between employment, saying at each, "So, what happened there?"

Peter could not say, *I was in rehab. My wife was divorcing me. I'm a recovering alcoholic. I overslept my shifts. I snuck drinks on the job.* Instead, he said, "Oh, you know how it is. This blasted economy."

"Mm-hmm," Tony grunted in return. After that, no matter what Peter offered—his unique recipe for rye, his years in customer service—he knew he'd lost Tony. He could feel his face turning red, his body growing hot with shame and frustration. He was leaning forward too much, over-gesticulating with his hands.

"Well, thanks for coming in." Tony dismissed him too soon, long before Peter had really gotten started. "We'll give you a call if we're interested."

"All right. Great. Sure thing. I'm looking forward to it."

They had one more handshake to cap things off, which Tony cut short as well, and then Peter was ejected from the bakery still a jobless loser. The counter girl didn't even look at him as he tried to smile at her on his way out. Bitch.

Outside in the street, the midday blues were starting— the time when things were too hot and too heavy, and all Peter wanted was to be unconscious. He would kill for a drink. The glare of the sun on the faces of passers-by seemed to wash everything out. It was like they were bleached of color and the will to live.

It didn't go that badly, Peter tried to tell himself, but he knew it was a lie.

BIANCA WAS KEEPING herself busy planning for Sam's future. Her only daughter had almost been lost but now she was back, and Bianca would devote the rest of her life to helping Sam recover if that was what it took. Sam had only gone through with the divorce six months before the accident. This was her chance to thrive, but Peter was always hovering about, hoping, no doubt, that Sam would change her mind and take him back.

Sam wouldn't, especially if Bianca had anything to say about it.

"Hi, Peter. How are things?" Bianca would greet him,

carefully and cordially, when he came to visit. He seemed to be intent on making amends, on getting his life together, but Bianca was wary and watched him like a hawk. If he made a move on her little girl, if he got too close and tried to hurt her—

Bianca could well remember the events that had precipitated the divorce. Sam had called her in the middle of the night, sobbing as she asked for a place to stay.

"You can always stay here, sweetie. You know that," Bianca had said, keeping her voice stable, steady, and devoid of judgment—though she certainly had plenty.

When Sam showed up at her door she'd had scratches on her leg from broken glass. She hadn't explained the injury, and Bianca hadn't asked.

"I hate him, Mom. He's such a bastard," Sam had cried, and Bianca had held her. She'd been reassuring and empathetic. She'd been motherly as she listened while Sam colored Peter's name with insults and then tried to take them back later, once her tears had dried. "He didn't really mean it," she'd insisted. "He's just so mean when he's drunk."

"And when *isn't* he drunk?" Bianca had countered, bitter and not bothering to hide it.

"He was doing good for a while."

Empty promises, Bianca had thought, and indeed, he'd called the next morning and promised to reform.

"Take a break from it, Sam. Stay a while with us. Think of it as giving him a chance to prove himself."

It had worked at first. Sam had stayed with Bianca for two whole months, precious time that had allowed a mother to re-bond with her daughter. Sam had grown into a truly remarkable woman. She was smart and spirited, independent and motivated. They'd had many conversations, long into the night, about how Sam could move her life forward if she wanted to, and Sam had finally made the decision—had made up her own mind, so she wouldn't back out. She'd found a place of her own and gone through with the divorce, and then when she'd been starting to move on with her own life, the accident had happened, and Peter had reappeared. Just like that, all of Sam's new opportunities had been snatched from her grasp.

Sam was a smart girl, but she'd given too much of herself away already. Bianca wasn't going to let her make the same mistake twice.

CHAPTER THIRTEEN

JIMMY HAD CREATED one simple rule for himself: never get attached to the cats. That didn't mean he didn't love them, but that he loved them with the understanding that, someday, he'd have to tell each and every single one of them goodbye. Most of them, if it were their good fortune, would get adopted. Others would leave the shop on another vehicle: death.

The new kittens were delightful, all crawly and tiny and warm. Only poor little Mickey wasn't allowed to suck her mamma's teat, which gave Jimmy the cause to bottle-feed her.

"There you go, Mickey," he'd say as he nursed her. "There you go. Get big and strong. Then you'll show 'em who's boss."

He could tell right away that Mickey had a personality. Even before she'd opened her eyes she's been as fiery as a firecracker. She was demanding and certain. She knew what she wanted, and had an intelligence and lucidity that Jimmy didn't often see in other cats.

"Okay, Mickey," he'd say when she signaled she was ready to be fed. "Just hang on, I'll get to it!"

Eventually, her colors started to show, and she was orange with a white star on her forehead. The mark reminded Jimmy a little of Annie Lenox. Jimmy toyed briefly with the idea of changing Mickey's name—*Come here, Annie*—but it was too sweet. Mickey was more appropriate; it had more of a bite to it and seemed to better suit the little orange fireball.

In the evenings Jimmy would play guitar and sing the songs that came to his mind. *As he came into the window, it was the sound of a crescendo…* He'd imagine each cat knew its part and would chime in when he got to the artist who was their namesake. Cats were funny about music. They mostly didn't sync up with it. They were too independent, but they still had their preferences. He could tell what they liked and what they didn't.

Sometimes Jimmy could get Mickey to come and sit next to him as he played. He liked the audience, and so he'd sit in the big chair by the doorway and get Mickey to lounge on the table at his side. They'd look out together over the crowd and serenade the feline beasts. Jimmy sang and Mickey watched him sing. She was hard to read, that one. Jimmy couldn't tell if she liked it or not. It was like she was analyzing, assessing. Like she hadn't made up her mind. Jimmy could tell she was strong-minded, so he didn't want to push it. Let her decide what she wanted. Jimmy could sit and sing all night.

PETER WAS THRILLED. He must have misread Tony; the bakery called him the next day with a job offer and now he was getting everything in order. He'd promised the landlord the rent check was coming soon—with interest. He was cleaning up.

When Sam was ready to live again, he'd be ready for her, too.

The next couple of weeks passed in a breeze. Peter was busy—going to the bakery, learning recipes for different types of bread, tidying up at home. Still, having explained the situation with his new boss, he found time to visit Sam at the hospital every day. Peter truly believed his visits helped.

"Hey there, Sammy," he greeted Sam at each visit. "Want to hear some Bowie?" And he'd queue it up on his phone and hold it next to her head, watching with rapt attention at the expressions that came over her face. She was still lying there inert, but her eyes were open and the music seemed to provoke eye movement. Sometimes her gaze flitted rapidly around the room. Once there was a chin toss, a lurch. He could feel the others in the room— the doctors and nurses, even the other patients—watching him, judging his choices, but they didn't know Sam like he did. He knew how to get his Sammy to dance.

It was two months of this treatment before Peter saw any real progress. In a way, that was good, he thought, because it gave him time to settle down. He'd lost ten pounds since he'd stopped drinking and Sam had been slimming up, too. That was what happened when you couldn't sit up and eat and all of your nourishment came through an IV. The rest of Sam's family still visited intermittently, and Bianca was almost always there, but it was Peter who was proving he could be reliable, day after day after day.

In the final week of October, Peter arrived to find Sam sitting upright in bed. She wasn't doing anything, and she was completely unattended—not even Bianca was in the hospital room at this hour. Peter tried to control the anxious fluttering in his chest as he walked to Sam's bedside in a manner that he hoped was cheerful and confident. He hadn't seen Madeline again, and for that he was grateful.

He should have brought flowers. He should have *known*. Goddamn it!

"Hey there, Sammy. How's the weather today?" Peter said, trying for casual. This had been another of their old jokes, the thing about the weather. Sam had liked to describe her emotional state in terms such as, *It's raining today*, if she was gloomy, or else, if there was hope, *It's cloudy, but there might be a chance of sun.*

Sam's eyes did not register any change in the room at all. Of course, Peter was used to her ignoring him. She still wasn't fully present, and though her eyes were always watching in a strange, unseeing way she hadn't really seen him come in. He sat at the head of the bed and placed his shoulder bag on the floor, then leaned forward and took Sam's right hand in both of his, clasping it.

"Hey," he said. When she didn't look at him, Peter massaged the tips of his fingers into her palm while running his thumbs over the back of her hand, hoping to trigger some sensation. He was so concentrated on massaging Sam's hand that the swift movement of her left arm took him by surprise. When her hand grasped him at his upper shoulder he could feel her fingers—cold—tighten urgently as they moved to the skin of his neck.

Sam's head swiveled and her eyes bore into his with an expression Peter didn't recognize. It was like she was seeing something past his eyes—like she was looking inside of him rather than at him, and she didn't like what she saw. "I'm hungry," Sam rasped, and Peter felt his throat constrict. Something about her voice was off. It wasn't just that it was huskier—that much was to be expected when someone had barely spoken in months—it was the intonation, the lilt of the words had changed from what he remembered. It wasn't Sam's voice.

"Okay, Sammy, okay," he said, releasing her right hand so he could remove the other gripping his neck. He placed both back down on the bedcovers and patted them gently. It must take time, he thought, this whole waking up process. He could understand that. She'd been through a lot. Now was his chance to show her how patient he could be, how cheerful and normal and stable. How *husbandly*. "How about we find you something to eat," he offered, stretching a reassuring smile across his face.

CHAPTER FOURTEEN

NOVEMBER HAD ARRIVED. Madeline knew she was letting too much time go by without visiting Sam, but she hadn't been able to make herself go back to the hospital since that day in late August. She didn't want to run into Peter or the rest of Sam's family and be forced to make small talk or, worse, explain herself. Besides, Madeline felt like it was all too much. The amount of constant attention Sam was getting had to be smothering her. And it was too much for Madeline, too. Run-ins with the ex-husband and the family were not something she was seeking. She also didn't see what she could do for Sam; it wasn't like Sam even knew Madeline was there while she was unconscious.

Instead, Madeline had been channeling all of her unsatisfied desire into her ghost story, as if the act of writing could put an end to the tension she wanted to avoid. She was writing a happy ending, forcing events to play out in the way that she wanted—the way they *weren't* going currently in reality but that they *could*, she was certain. Yet, night after night she woke up in a sweat. The morning she decided to go back to the hospital was no different. She'd been caught up in another intense dream about Sam.

"We can't stay here," Sam had said in the dream.

They'd been in Sam's house by the lake—the one

Madeline had conjured up in her mind, since she'd never been there in real life—embracing in the dining room, swaying to music, somewhat drunk.

"Why not?" asked Madeline. Ignoring Sam's protests, she'd pushed the other woman against the wall as desire overtook her. Sam had groped for the lights, and then everything went dark. Madeline could hear Sam's breathing, loud and clear in the dream. She could feel the physical presence of Sam's warmth in front of her. She could smell her skin, patchouli and musk.

In the dream, Madeline ran her hands under Sam's shirt, her fingers sliding around her waist. They'd skip the bedroom. They'd do it right there. Pressing Sam against the wall she fiddled with the button of Sam's jeans. Sam growled encouragingly in her ear.

I'm hungry. I'm going to eat you up. Sam's eyes flashed in the darkness, but it wasn't really Sam's eyes. They were different—they were ravenous, diseased. Bottomless.

Suddenly the struggle was different. The body against Madeline's wasn't Sam. Madeline needed to get away. She writhed and pulled but was caught by the person that had once been Sam. "Help!" Madeline cried, trying to scream out around Sam's hand, which was covering her mouth, making her breath stale while the other grabbed at her throat, choking off her words.

"Help!" Madeline's scream into the room was silent and she woke up moaning, still trying to get out the word, *"Hellll—"*

Madeline sucked in a deep breath and tried to calm down. It was early morning and still dark, but she could hear birds chirping outside. The way Sam had touched her in the dream had felt wrong, but... Madeline slid her hands into her underwear and tried to reimagine the scene, to make it good, to make it the fantasy it could be. There was no monster this time, just Sam as she remembered—willing and wanting. Madeline moved her hips, imagining Sam's lips and eyes. Her tongue, her fingers, her nose, her breath.

"Sam," Madeline shuddered, but her orgasm was weak and left her unsatisfied.

Afterward, she felt empty, but no longer scared.

Madeline got up. She pulled on clean clothes. She ruffled her hair, checked the weather, and made up her mind to visit Sam. It was only November, but already the sky was threatening snow.

THE HUMAN CALLED Peter was leaning close, helping the ghost to stand. It wrapped its arms around Peter's neck. As it had gained control over its new shell over the past months it had grown to know the different humans. It had become more comfortable in its own human body, though many things were still unclear.

"I'm hungry," the ghost said, using this most familiar and immediate of phrases. It had discovered a wealth of language stored in its memory that it could recall easily enough and make use of when necessary, but most was irrelevant. What it needed was food.

"Yeah, yeah. Okay," said Peter. "It wouldn't hurt, you know, to say, 'hi,' or, 'glad to see you'." The ghost looked at Peter and Peter looked at the ghost. Peter was the first to look away. "Forget it. Let's go find you something to eat."

The ghost supported its weight on Peter's arm as they moved down the hallway to find the metal box that slid between the walls of this place. The elevator would take them down, down, to the lowest floor where the food was kept. A human woman in a hairnet would put food on the tray, while the ghost would stare at her with barely-concealed lust. She was fat and her body oozed oil and sugar. She would taste wonderfully fried—the fat would crisp, the meat would be tender and sweet. Her skin was smooth, unblemished, and faintly red at the cheeks. She had full lips and a thick neck. Naked, the ghost imagined, she'd be like a bowl of blood pudding. Just remove the skin and dive into the contents beneath.

The ghost's legs were still wobbly as it walked down the hallway. Its limbs were unpredictable, and it occasionally lost feeling in one foot. It was infuriating. It needed to go faster. It needed to eat. It needed to stuff this body full.

"Hey there, easy, just—careful of my hand, I just—*fuck*!" Peter cried as the ghost stumbled, using his hand to stop its fall.

Without warning, the ghost was pushed against the

wall. Peter held it firmly, his breathing hard and uneven. His fingers were digging into its shoulders in ten hard points. In Peter's eyes, the ghost saw something.

Hunger, it realized.

Hunger for something—from the ghost, from its body. From whomever the body had belonged to before it the ghost had claimed it.

Peter's hunger was driving him toward a cliff and at the bottom would be the ghost. It would wait for him to fall with its mouth open. It licked its lips in anticipation.

Peter released the ghost's shoulders and shook himself like he was trying to shake off the hunger, but the ghost knew he couldn't—it was too deep inside of him. "I'm sorry," he said. "It's just…my hand. I burned it yesterday in the bakery—" He pulled the ghost roughly back into the middle of the hall, reattaching it to his arm as two humans walked toward them, one wearing a hospital gown exactly like the one the ghost wore.

"Hi there," Peter said as they passed, his voice higher as he inclined his head, making the shape with his mouth that was a smile as he tried to pull the ghost along, gently now, in the direction of the cafeteria.

The ghost had seen him. It had seen his true side, and his true side was dangerous. The ghost clung to Peter more willingly now. If it stayed close, it might be able to…

"Oh—," Peter said, stopping suddenly. "Madeline."

When the ghost looked down the hall again it saw a third human approaching. This one was small without much flesh on its bones, but faintly familiar... had the ghost seen this one before?

As SOON AS Madeline saw Sam with Peter, she knew something was wrong.

Sam was walking now, which should have been good, but she was staring at everything with a dull, longing expression. It was cold, angry. Ravenous. Madeline had a chilling flashback to her nightmare. The Sam she had known never looked at anything like that.

Peter was beside her, looking jumpy and guilty, awkward and uncomfortable. What was he up to? Was he hiding something? Did he think things would be different now between him and Sam?

"We were just going to the cafeteria," Peter said when their paths were in danger of converging and he had to acknowledge her or be obviously rude. "Want to join us?"

"Uh, yeah," Madeline agreed, even though of course she didn't, and he must have known that, but she had no choice. She couldn't very well have said, *I think I'll pass*, though she wanted to.

They walked back in the direction Madeline had come, summoned the elevator, and waited in silence. Madeline tried to breathe normally, tried to moderate her emotions. This felt wrong and bad, but the reason why eluded her.

"It looks like snow out there," Peter observed blandly.

"Uh, yeah," Madeline said again, and then she searched desperately for something else to say. "Winter's coming."

Peter laughed, and it sounded unnatural. Forced. "Yeah. Better watch out. Santa will be here before you know it."

The elevator arrived and the doors opened much too slowly, as if they dreaded letting in ill-fated passengers. Ignoring the feeling, Madeline shuttled herself through the doors, followed by Peter and then, moving sluggishly, Sam.

Inside, Madeline and Peter flanked the woman they had both coveted for so long, though whether it was to use her as a barrier between them or to keep her protected, Madeline wasn't sure. The halves of the door stood resolutely open for at least ten seconds before they slowly inched closed. When they finally did Madeline felt the pressure of suffocation immediately.

Peter hit the button for floor "B" repeatedly, but the elevator didn't move. "Damn thing," he muttered, and half a minute later everything heaved into motion with a deep sigh. From floor four, down to three... Madeline could feel Sam's presence at her shoulder, but she hardly dared to turn and look. Instead, she stole a glimpse out of the corner of her eye.

Sam was staring at her, but her eyes were hard and cruel.

Madeline quickly averted her gaze as goosebumps raised over her skin. She had no way to decode the look in Sam's eyes, and she didn't like what it might mean.

Ever so softly, Sam's arm brushed against Madeline's and she pulled away, removing the contact. Sam's body was emitting some kind of strange, nauseating energy that was palpable and thick in the confined space. Where Madeline had once felt pulled into Sam's brightness, now all she wanted was to get away—to run and never look back. She never should have come to the hospital. There was a reason she had stayed away. She hadn't known what it was at first—and she still wasn't totally sure she could articulate it—but it had something to do with Sam and what had become of her.

At last, they arrived at the cafeteria level. The elevator beeped and the doors shuddered open. The aroma of hot food filled the air and Sam launched herself forward, making for the lunch buffet, behind which a fat woman stood sweating under her hairnet.

"Hey!" Peter called out, hurrying out after Sam. Madeline trailed behind, giving them space. There was an old man in the line in front of them, loading up on potatoes. The fat woman turned to Sam, and her eyes widened in recognition.

"Hello," she said. "Some of everything again?"

"All of it," Sam barked out in a strange, hoarse voice.

"Yeah, yeah. A little of everything. That's all you can have, honey. This here is all we've got."

Sam's eyes moved in tandem with the woman's spoon as she watched the woman pile scoops of various dishes onto her plate, urging her for "more, more." The end result was a tray heaped with a gross quantity of food, but Sam still appeared dissatisfied. She grabbed the tray and then rushed for the nearest table where she sat heavily and immediately began shoveling food into her mouth, ignoring the plastic utensils and making do with her hands.

"Hey, easy!" Peter said as he tried to coax a fork into Sam's fingers. After thirty seconds of struggling, Peter gave up, backing off, hands in the air in surrender. He glanced at Madeline as if looking for help.

"Has she been like this long?" Madeline couldn't hide her shock.

"Ever since she woke up. I'm pretty sure she recognizes me, but sometimes I don't know. It's like she has a one-track mind, and it's trained on food. No one can get her to focus on physical therapy unless we promise to feed her something after she's cooperated. She's like an infant or an animal, except obviously she's not…"

Madeline watched Sam cram food into her mouth, and the comparison to an animal wasn't too far off. It was a terrible thing to think, and Madeline didn't want to, but this just wasn't Sam. It wasn't her at all. The woman at the table was a stranger.

"What about language?" asked Madeline, knowing how important the topic was to Sam, particularly as a professor. "Is she talking? Reading?"

"Reading?" Peter scoffed. "Maybe we could try a cookbook, but otherwise, not a chance in hell. She can talk okay, but she doesn't have much to say. Just, 'I'm hungry!

When's lunch?'" Peter's voice affected a hoarse tone that was eerily reminiscent of Sam's new voice. "She's like a damn garbage disposal," he went on. "I'm surprised she hasn't thrown up all over me, given the amount she eats."

Even as he said it, Sam began to gag and Madeline wondered if Sam had thrown up on *other* things, just not Peter. Sam paused, mouth open as her throat moved visibly in a hard swallow that looked like she was forcing a mass through a much smaller pipe, and then, after a big burp and a momentarily satisfied smile, she continued to shovel in the food as ravenously as before.

Peter studied Sam's rounded spine, her swelling stomach. "Sometimes I wonder," he said, watching Sam, not Madeline, "if this is some sort of a sick joke, like some kind of payback."

"Payback? For what?"

"Oh, come on. I'm sure she's told you." There was a hint of derision in Peter's tone.

Madeline waited, thinking she probably did know what Peter meant, but also not wanting to put any words in his mouth.

Peter sighed. "The alcohol. The fact that I let it ruin our marriage. The fact that I couldn't stop myself, I just *had* to have it, and so now she's doing it back to me, but she's doing it with food. Making herself sick. Showing me how it feels to see someone do that."

"Oh, come on," said Madeline. "Sam wouldn't do that."

"You don't know Sam," Peter countered, "not like I do. Did. She could be bitter, vengeful. We both could. We brought out the worst in each other." He stopped for a moment and seemed to consider his words. "I don't want to think it's true, but it could be something subconscious, like this huge suppressed anger that's finally boiling over in a massive, self-destructive act that was somehow triggered by her waking up and seeing me there…" His voice wandered off, leaving Madeline to fill in the rest.

Madeline felt uncomfortable hearing Peter talk like this about Sam when she was sitting right there.

"Still," argued Madeline, "if it were that, couldn't you talk to her? And besides, you look… I mean, how are you doing?"

Peter looked at Madeline. His face was tired and worn, his eyes glassy and deep and sad. "Do you mean am I drinking myself to sleep every night? No. I mean, I am, just with chamomile tea."

"Chamomile?"

"It's supposed to help you sleep. Mostly it makes me have to pee, so I think it might be doing the reverse. Think I should let the advertising companies know? Their slogan should really be, *Chamomile! Wakes you up at night to pee!*" Peter looked eagerly at Madeline, waiting for a reaction. "What, you don't think I should take that one onstage? Don't worry. Sam wouldn't either. You two are a lot alike. Isn't that right, Sammy?" Peter asked, raising his voice and addressing her directly in a tone that bordered on sarcastic. "You don't think I'm the next Robin Williams?"

Sam had cleared all the food on the tray and was licking her fingers. When that was done, she picked up the tray and licked it, too, until the entire thing was covered with a sheen of clear spit.

Madeline wasn't sure what to say, and so she let the silence hang between them. One thought kept returning to her mind that she was trying to push down, but the more she watched Sam, the harder it was to ignore. *She's so hungry, it's like she's possessed.*

"She's getting better, don't you think?" asked Peter, looking at Madeline hopefully.

"Yeah," Madeline lied, "sure she is."

CHAPTER FIFTEEN

PETER HADN'T MEANT to grab Sam in the hallway like that. It had been a reflex. She'd grabbed his hand where he had burned it and it triggered some buried rage, but the expression in her eyes when he'd pinned her was unfazed. There was no fear, no anger. No usual pissed off Sam. The closest word he had for the look might have been desire, but it wasn't that, either.

It was more encompassing somehow—a chasm that could never be filled. And it looked almost eager.

When Peter jerked off later, he found himself recalling that look in Sam's eyes. His breath caught, and he came in a pitiful shudder that didn't leave him satisfied. At least the urge to masturbate had come back to him now that he'd quit the booze. That was something.

A few days later, when Peter arrived at the hospital for his visit, he ran into Bianca. Sam wasn't in the room. She'd probably been taken for a quick exam. Peter was relieved Sam's dad, Jeff, wasn't there with Bianca. Jeff had never gotten along with Peter, despite the large amount of effort Peter had put in to sucking up to him—watching the Dodgers together even though he didn't like the Dodgers or baseball—and cooking hamburgers on the grill out back.

"Hi, Bianca."

"Oh, hi, Peter," Bianca said with her usual aridness. She looked tired, but her smile was automatic. She was built broader and sturdier than Sam and had always struck Peter as being a bit masculine, even though Sam was the tomboy. Bianca had dyed auburn hair that fell in curls to her cheekbones, and she always looked put-together and professional. "How's work?" she asked. "Sam tells me you got a new job."

"She does?" Peter stumbled for a moment, forgetting, momentarily, that Sam could speak. "I mean, I do. It's good. I'm working at the new bakery on Wentworth, and it's steady. Pays the rent." Peter had not yet heard Sam string together much in the way of coherent sentences, but it made sense that her mom would be the one to get her to talk and that it would, of course, be to gossip about him.

Bianca nodded. "Good, good. I'm glad to hear it. Do you have plans for the holidays?"

Again, Peter stumbled. He'd nearly forgotten Thanksgiving was right around the corner. The weather outside had been bitterly cold but there had been no real snow yet, just a few flakes that hadn't stuck.

"I haven't really thought about it."

"Well, if the doctors are right and Sam is released in time, Jeff and I are planning on having a celebration in her honor. You should come," Bianca said, and then she seemed to catch herself. She looked guiltily at Peter and then away, adding, "Madeline should come, too. Everyone should come! Everyone who's helped out, I mean, since the accident…" She trailed off, leaving an awkward silence in the space between them.

"Yeah?" Peter said. He doubted Bianca really wanted him there, but he wasn't about to miss out on what might be his one chance to make amends with Sam's family. "Sure, that would be great! I mean, if she's…"

Sam shuffled back into the room using a walker. Instead of a hospital gown, she was dressed in her own pajamas, a mismatched set that Peter recognized from years before— blue drawstring pants and an oversized tee shirt that said "Get Lit" on the cover of a book. She said nothing and made no eye contact with anyone as she sat back down on the bed and swung her legs in front of her, pulling the sheets over them. Only then did she turn to her mother and say, in that now-familiar raspy whisper, "I'm hungry."

"I thought you would be, love," Bianca said, extracting a sandwich and a granola bar from her bag, then unwrapping the first and holding it out for Sam to take. Sam grabbed it and stuffed it into her mouth as if she hadn't eaten in months. That was just how she always ate these days. Bianca was already unwrapping the granola bar in preparation.

As Sam ate, her eyes drifted to Peter. Finishing one half of the sandwich, she paused, licked the tips of her fingers, and then whispered as she lifted the second half to her mouth. "I'm hungry." Sam's gaze held his and something about the way she said it made Peter think it had nothing to do with ham and cheese. His stomach lurched.

"No, dear," Bianca said in a cheerful, motherly voice—the kind reserved for young children and not grown women. "You mean, 'I'm eating,' or, 'I'm getting full,' or maybe even, 'This is good'." Bianca patted Sam's leg under the sheets and turned to Peter, shaking her head. "She still gets confused, but don't worry. It'll just take time."

EVER SINCE THEIR encounter in the hallway the ghost had been watching Peter carefully during his visits. When everyone had left and the ghost was alone again it lay in bed fantasizing about the people that had visited. Bianca was an excellent provider of food. Peter, on the other hand, was mostly a nuisance. Yet, there was darkness in him the ghost could identify with, and he seemed to have given a great deal of power over to whoever it was that had inhabited this body. With a little push, the ghost might be able to get Peter to give himself completely to the ghost. The thought sent a thrill of desire through the ghost's body.

It could hardly wait.

BIANCA WANTED TO generate as much support as she could for Sam during her recovery, which was why she was hosting the Thanksgiving party.

At first, Jeff had opposed it, especially the part about inviting Peter and Madeline.

"Just keep it to family," he'd argued over dinner. "Or invite some of Sam's friends, if you want to. But Peter? He's been clinging to Sam for so long, and Christ, I wish we could just ship him off to some other planet and never have to deal with him again. They're *divorced*, Bianca, why invite him?"

"I don't know…" Bianca mused, grasping for a reason to explain why she'd been compelled to invite him. "He's just been around so much lately. I guess I've gotten used to him."

She looked apologetically at Jeff who snorted and shook his head.

"That man has no future—zilch," he said. "He's just bogged down by a long history he wants back."

"Like Gatsby." The words came out of Bianca's mouth automatically. Peter was certainly no Jay Gatsby, but the undeniable similarity was in the desire to reclaim a past that was dead and gone.

"What?"

Bianca shook her head. "Nothing." She sighed and raised one hand to push back hair that was falling in her face. "Look, I hear what you're saying, and maybe you're right. But the problem is, I already invited him."

"What?" Jeff's eyes widened.

"It just slipped out." Bianca shrugged. "Reflex. He was there at the hospital last week, and the poor sap seemed so lonely—"

Jeff snorted again, interrupting his wife's excuses. "Bianca, you're as bad as Sam is! You two think it's your job to save everyone."

"Well, maybe he won't come." Bianca resolutely set down her fork and stood to clear away their empty plates. It wasn't what she'd planned. She was trying to protect Sam, but it had been difficult since she'd woken up. Her daughter wasn't the same now as she had been before, though it was hard to say how exactly. Peter was willing to do so much, and God knew she could use an extra pair of hands.

CHAPTER SIXTEEN

THANKSGIVING HIT BOSTON cold and hard. The sky finally made true on its threat and snowed. Pedestrians scurried about the streets, wrapped in long coats and fuzzy hats, their gloved hands stuffed into pockets and heads bent against the wind as they navigated around icy patches of the ground.

Jimmy watched them pass outside his shop as he played holiday tunes over the speakers. Some people got upset if you played Christmas tunes before Thanksgiving was over, but Jimmy had always had a soft spot for the magic of the Christmas season. After all, Santa was kind of like Christ, when you got down to it, wasn't he? There was the baby in the manger and the man with the presents. Weren't they really kind of connected? Wasn't Santa just a stand-in for God?

The holidays were about hope, Jimmy thought, and he tried to surround himself with it. Not to mention, in a world like this one, he needed all the hope he could get. Everybody did.

Jimmy scratched Mickey under the chin. "You're happy here, aren't you, little girl?" he asked. She lifted her chin, closed her eyes, and purred. "Do you want to get adopted, or do you want to stay here with old Jimmy?" He used both hands, massaging the sides of her tiny face as he spoke. "Do you want to grow up big and strong, and be the ruler of this whole domain? The queen?" The kitten shook back and forth in delight as he rubbed her little body. Picking her up, Jimmy tucked Mickey into the crook of his arm, continuing to pet her. Her purring formed the background music for his thoughts. He'd promised himself he'd never get attached to the cats, but Mickey was so different. He couldn't help but feel his heart softening for her.

What was Jimmy thankful for? For snow, he thought, watching it fall outside the window, and for the cats—especially Mickey.

PETER CURSED THE flakes falling outside the window of his apartment. The high for Thanksgiving Day was predicted to reach twenty-five, but by evening things were expected to fall to the negatives. He put on long underwear first, followed by his nicest pair of jeans, a white undershirt, a pinstriped shirt, and a blue bowtie. He could do this, Peter thought to himself as he smoothed down his hair and adjusted his collar. He could go to Bianca's, where he'd gone so many times before. He could mingle with Sam's family, he could be cordial to Madeline if she showed, and he could not drink a drop. Not a single drop, unless it was only a sip of champagne to toast, and even then only if someone offered, so as not to be rude. Or, if Jeff and the guys had that special brew from Vermont, the kind in the can. That was tradition, and how could a man say no to tradition?

Warm anticipation started in Peter as he thought of cracking open a can, but he caught himself. He knew where he'd wind up if he let himself go there, and these were slippery thoughts. He could see his mom's face, he could feel his dad's absence, and Sam…first her tears, then that strange, stony look that had ultimately replaced them. She'd hardened herself because of him. His soft, loving Sammy had gone colder than any beer he'd ever had.

Taking a deep breath, Peter sighed and stared meaningfully at his own face in the mirror. He'd made it three months without a drink, but he'd made it this far before. It was always around now that he'd manage to slip up—which meant there was the possibility he'd slip again. There'd be a party or a get-together, and he'd think, "I can take it or I can leave it," and then, of course, he'd take it.

He always did.

"It's now or never," Peter whispered fiercely at himself. Even after these few sober months he still had a drunk's face—a drunk's papery skin and broken-capillary-blistered nose. "You can do this. You succeed, or you kill yourself. For real. No more failing. This is your last chance."

Bianca was still in her running around clothes when her

daughter-in-law, Carly, arrived with her granddaughters. Bianca had spent the day before cleaning, and the afternoon had been consumed with decorations and food. She shivered when the cold air followed the girls in the door. Of course, the first snow would arrive on Thanksgiving.

"Go on girls, stomp your boots. Get it all off." Carly raised her head and turned her attention to her mother-in-law. Carly was a good wife to Tom, Bianca thought. Smart. Energetic. "We've been having a bit of a rough day," Carly said, motioning at her daughters with fatigue obvious on her face, "but I brought tons of toys to see if we can't cheer them up."

"Well, hello, my little loves!" Bianca cooed. She knelt down and smothered her granddaughters in hugs, then lowered her voice so she could disclose a secret without their mother hearing. "I've got fresh cookies in the oven, and the first two will go to you!" She was in her element with the young ones. She'd taught fourth grade for over thirty years, but she loved them more when they were even younger, wide-eyed and delectable, demanding and innocent, their cheeks pink from cold and with fluffy little hats on their heads. Six years old and four, the girls were Rosa and Diane—an odd, mature name for the youngest. Rosa was dark-haired and skeptical-mouthed and reminded Bianca of Sam, and indeed, Sam had taken quite a hand in helping both of them develop into fierce little feminists. "I'm sure Sam will be thrilled to see them.

Maybe they can speak her language better than the rest of us can. Where's Tom?" Bianca straightened up to her feet, turning to Carly.

"He took the car back out to pick up groceries," Carly said as she hoisted up Rosa, who had been tugging at her shirt. "Is this what you've made so far?" she asked, motioning to the two dishes of salad, a basket of rolls, and a pie sitting on the counter by the stove.

Bianca smiled proudly. "Some of it. I've got cookies in the oven and the rest is out back in the other room, where Jeff's cooling the drinks." As she walked, Bianca took Rosa by the hand and guided Carly to the sunroom. When they arrived at the buffet table set opposite the snow-covered garden outside, Carly eyed the feast and let out a short laugh.

"Oh my. I should tell Tom not to bother with groceries after all. We could probably eat for a week with all of this and never run out of food!"

"Maybe, but more doesn't hurt," Bianca beamed, wiping her hands on her apron. She took Rosa's little fingers and wiped off the stickiness on them, too. "What did you get into? What's all over your hands?" Bianca asked the girl, squatting down to her level.

Rosa avoided Bianca's eyes, a shy smile spreading across her face as she dug into the pockets of her jeans and pulled out a small handful of bright candies.

"Skittles," she said, showing her grandmother the brightly colored candy. The sugar coating was melting, leaving trails of red, orange, and green on her small palm. Rosa let them slip back into her pocket, all except one—a yellow one—which she popped into her mouth before licking her hand thoroughly with her tongue. The girl had always had a sweet tooth.

"Not before dinner," Bianca scolded lightly, taking the hand and wiping it off again. "And you'll destroy your pants. Come with me and we can find a better place to keep those."

"Is Sam here yet?" Carly asked, the edge of her voice laced with hesitancy. "I haven't seen her in ages...not since she was just barely conscious. She seemed a little zombie-like back then, though."

Bianca knew Carly meant no harm by her comment, so she tried not to let it bother her. She'd been mentally preparing for this since she brought Sam home last week, and she'd just have to face the reactions that were coming—the stares, the whispers, and the judgment she was sure would fill their eyes.

CHAPTER SEVENTEEN

"PETER!"

Bianca's false cheer was so convincing that Peter almost believed it. He accepted her embrace with goodwill as he stepped through the open door and into Sam's parents' house. "What can I get you to drink? We have soda, juice, seltzer with lime…"

"Lime and seltzer would be great," he said, followed with an obligatory, "Happy Thanksgiving."

"To you, too," Bianca returned, sweeping gracefully into the kitchen and away from him. The house smelled delicious—of cinnamon and apples and roasted turkey. The cheer of it made Peter choke up. In a way, this had once belonged to him. These people, this home—they had once been his family, too. It was terrible how a divorce could make you feel like only half of yourself, like all the best parts of you had been stripped away. Then again, Peter had never deserved those parts, anyway. He'd known that, and so had Sam. She'd probably always known it.

"Where is she?" he asked when Bianca brought him his drink, tall and fizzing, filled with ice and capped with a wedge of lime. He could have gone and helped her with it. He could have, but he hadn't. Strike one, Peter.

Bianca produced a patient smile and relinquished the

drink, but there was something behind her eyes Peter couldn't name. "At the table in the sunroom, eating appetizers. Want to follow me and grab one of those veggie trays?" she answered, moving away again. "I'm trying to encourage the girls to eat something in vegetable form."

Peter trotted into the kitchen and retrieved a tray of sliced carrots, cucumber, and cauliflower heads. "If you've got any toothpicks, I bet we could make them into a kind of sculpture..." he started, but Bianca had disappeared through the doorway, ignoring him.

She was busy, Peter consoled himself. Stressed. After dinner and a few drinks, she'd relax. She'd see he really was making a change—that he didn't bring anyone down now, because he was on his way up.

The room was filled with the noise of voices. Jeff was loud, and Sam's brother Tom was even louder. Both were laughing and moving in a way that indicated they were already aboard the happy train and on their way to Tipsyville, where everything was warm and the light was fuzzy and the beer tasted sweeter. Peter immediately felt emasculated in their presence, aware of the scrawniness of his arms and the roundness of his belly. It was hard not to see how much they must hate him clinging to Sam, a girl who could hold her own in an argument, drink beer with the guys, and make raunchy jokes that sent them all spinning.

Peter didn't measure up. Or, he *hadn't* measured up. He was different now.

When Peter saw Sam he noticed that she'd developed a scrawniness of her own. She sat hunched over in her chair, frantically shoveling handfuls of cheese into her mouth. There was an unmistakable roundness to her spine, but it seemed to affect her midsection alone. Her arms and shoulders were thin, almost emaciated, and with her stringy legs and bloated belly she looked one of those starving children on television with protruding stomachs. Peter thought—as he did every time he saw Sam eat—that there was something disturbingly animalistic about her. It was grotesque, but he still wanted her despite it. Peter wanted Sam desperately. He couldn't help it. She'd put on weight, but then hell, so had he. That didn't change who she was inside, did it?

Peter placed the tray of vegetables on the table in front of where the two younger girls were playing. "Look at this," he said, forcing his voice to sound excited over vegetables. "We've got some tasty treats here!"

Rosa perked up at that, lifting her head and craning her chin to get a look. Her attention was distracted, however, by Sam. "Why does she have to eat like that?" she demanded. "It's so gross!"

"Hey, be nice," said Peter, but Rosa had already returned to her game. He tried to catch Bianca's eye, to shrug, as in, *Kids! What can you do?* But she wasn't facing him, and all he was able to manage was a quick hello from Carly as she tried to monitor the girls' activities. He gave a wave and a nod to the men before assuming the place he really wanted to be: the open seat next to Sam.

"Hey, Sammy," he said, affecting a boisterous cheer. "Isn't this a happy Thanksgiving? You awake and all your family around to celebrate?"

Sam's father and brother glanced at Peter briefly before resuming their private conversation. This was the moment in the old days where he would have said, "Enjoying the brewskies?" and helped himself to a bottle, tipping into a carelessness that made socializing more fluid while he pretended at a machismo he picked up on by following the others' cues. Lean forward. Chest out. Smack the table.

It was kind of fun, posturing with the guys, once he got the hang of it, but it wasn't really him. And Sam had loved him because he *wasn't* them. He was just himself: an oddball doofus, a little bit sappy, and madly in love.

"I'll just steal a piece of this," Peter said, reaching for a toothpick to spear into a cube of cheddar. Sam's eyes tracked his hand as he took the piece, but otherwise her eating pattern was uninterrupted. She'd cleared away most of the cheese. There were only a few stray cubes at the edges of the tray, one of which Peter managed to stab. When he reached for a second, though, Sam grabbed for a toothpick, raised it menacingly, and bared her teeth at him.

"Okay, okay," Peter said, backing off. "Guess you must be hungry. It's all yours."

Sam consumed what was left of the cheese and then raised the tray to her mouth as she had in the hospital, licking away any traces that were left. Peter should probably have averted his eyes like the others, but he just stared, transfixed, tracking the movement of her tongue. What the hell had happened to her? It made him angry. This was so unlike Sam—she *had* to be fucking with them!

When she was finished with the tray, Sam's eyes lifted but didn't meet Peter's gaze. Instead, she looked his body up and down in a manner that gave Peter the unsettling sensation that he was a piece of meat and Sam the butcher. "Hungry," she whispered in her new throaty voice.

"Yes," Peter agreed. He gulped and tried to swallow away the fear that had threatened to eclipse his anger. There was nothing to be afraid of. Sam was just still recovering. "I'm hungry, too. I've hardly eaten all day."

Sam released the tray and reached for Peter. Instinctively, he pulled back, his fear rushing up his throat like vomit. His retreat was buffered by the arrival of Bianca, Carly, and Tom, who arrived in the room carrying steaming dishes of turkey and gravy and mashed potatoes.

"Time to eat," Bianca cheered, oblivious to the sudden tension between Sam and Peter. "Get it while it's hot!"

This proved to be a distraction for both Peter and Sam, and they tucked into the food with vigor. Peter rarely cooked for himself. It was a real treat to eat home cooking, especially after months of microwave dinners and bachelor takeout. The turkey was tender and juicy, the gravy thick, and the potatoes fluffy. The green bean casserole was crispy and creamy, though the corn was a little too buttery, not that anyone would mind. The only thing that would have made it better would have been a drink with a little kick to it, something to round out the flavors of the food. The lime seltzer Bianca had prepared for him was too fizzy. It lacked substance. Peter did his best to ignore it, concentrating on the food.

"How's work?" Tom asked, and Peter perked up between bites to describe how well he was doing at his new job and how he was getting along with his colleagues, and banking some overtime as well.

"I made some kickass rye bread—Sammy's old favorite—and they fell all over themselves to use it in the shop. Maybe one of these days I can have my own bakery and really show 'em how it's done."

"That's great," Bianca said, grinning broadly with her teeth, and Peter thought she might really be impressed. "We'll have to come by and get a loaf."

"I'll give you the employee discount." Peter punctuated the statement with his fork to show he was serious.

"Yes," Sam mumbled, a slight smile creeping along the edges of her lips. Peter looked at her in surprise.

"Yes, what?" Peter asked, leaning in and trying to catch her eye in his hope to draw something more substantial out of her. "Yes, you'll come to get some bread?"

Sam's smile froze and then vanished, leaving her face devoid of expression. She returned to her food without so much as another glance at him, and Peter sighed, trying to pick up the threads of the conversation that had already moved on without him.

CHAPTER EIGHTEEN

AFTER HER LAST visit with Sam, Madeline had experienced a chilling revelation, but she didn't want to accept it. The revelation was this: Sam was gone, and it was Madeline's fault. In a way, Sam was still here, because she was still talking and moving around. At the same time, it was clear to Madeline that the person she had known as Sam had been replaced by something else—something dark and deceitful. Something *deadly*, and disturbingly like the hungry ghost she was writing about.

Still, Madeline didn't want to jump to any conclusions about what it was that had replaced Sam. To think that writing a story about their lives could have such a dangerous impact bordered on psychotic, and Madeline didn't want to think she was insane.

So, instead she was sitting alone on her bed in her dark bedroom with her laptop on her legs, regretting her life choices and feeling indecisive. Bianca had invited her to Sam's Thanksgiving/Welcome Home party and Madeline thought maybe she should go, if for no other reason than to confirm her hunch about what might have happened to Sam.

Madeline had gotten dressed, but couldn't manage to get herself to leave the apartment. How could she go to

Sam's parents' house and pretend everything was fine? Could no one else see that Sam was going through more than just a spell of strangeness—that she herself was *changed*, maybe even replaced? Madeline wanted to see Sam, but she wanted nothing to do with whatever had woken up in Sam's place. She hated feeling helpless, and yet that was what she was. The only thing she seemed able to do was sit at her computer and write, even though that might have been what had caused all this trouble in the first place. Of course, that was simply another borderline crazy thought she didn't want to accept.

She reviewed the scene she'd been writing. Madeline had summoned the ghost into the world through her desperate words, but the happy ending she'd been striving for had vanished. In its place had come the grimmest version of the current situation—the one in which Sam was truly, irrevocably gone. In this new version of the story, the hungry ghost had taken possession of Sam and swallowed her whole as it did everything. The climax, Madeline realized, would happen on Thanksgiving—tonight. It was a feast after all. That was when the hungry ghost would get a chance to really *feed*.

But even though Madeline felt deep in her bones that something terrible and unavoidable was coming, she couldn't write about it. Events were building momentum, but she still couldn't see where they were headed. She was unable to finish the story, and try as she might she couldn't seem to fill the last empty pages.

To gain a little perspective, Madeline opened the window, packed the bowl of her glass pipe with freshly ground marijuana, and settled back onto her bed, smoking meditatively. A few minutes later she felt better, clearer, and more lucid. Whatever was going to happen would happen, and she needed to go and meet it—both the inevitable ending of the story and the woman that had once been her fantasy. It was, after all, just a story.

It was time to let them both go. But first, she had to go and see Sam, to see whether she was really gone or if there was still a way to save things, which meant she had to go and buy some wine. It wouldn't do to show up to Sam's party empty-handed.

Madeline threw on her coat, her hat, and her gloves, and then paused at the door to search for nearby liquor store options on her phone. Sam's parents lived near Harvard Square, and there was a liquor store still open not too far off her route that she could swing by. The detour shouldn't take her more than ten, maybe fifteen minutes. She'd be at the party in time for dessert.

The world outside was pulsing slightly, or maybe that was the result of the pot. As she stepped out into the winter storm, Madeline felt cleansed instantly of the stale inside air. Her first breath cleared her lungs; the second stung her nose.

Madeline walked, hands in her pockets, until she reached the subway to Harvard Square. The atmosphere was mostly one of high spirits. College kids swayed where they stood, and older couples walked together, carrying parcels in paper bags. Only a few people she saw seemed less than jovial, and those were the lone travelers in worn shoes, making their way to or from work on a commute that hadn't cared it was a holiday. Madeline tried not to feel guilty when she saw them, but she always did when she saw people unhappy. She had her struggles, but at the same time, she had it easy. Yeah, she'd fallen in love with a woman who'd gotten possessed or gone insane or something equally bizarre during a tragic accident-induced coma. Still, there were worse things that could happen.

Madeline exited the subway at Harvard Square with her eyes locked on her phone. She navigated familiar streets before finding herself in new territory, beyond the area of the bars that she frequented. Things seemed vaguely familiar as she passed little boutiques, a hole-in-the-wall crepe place, and a Tibetan artifacts shop. According to the map, the liquor store should be just around the corner, one more block south—not too far past Grendel's, actually.

She waited at the light. The few other people out and about seemed to be going in the opposite direction, and so when the light changed a cluster of people crossed one way while she crossed the other alone. Passing the corner shop, she noticed it had a funny name.

"*Jimmy's Used Cat Emporium*," Madeline read aloud, smirking. What a ridiculous name for a store. It was after seven p.m. on Thanksgiving, but the light in the shop was on, and the sign on the door said it was open. Christmas music was coming from inside, and within dozens of cats roamed freely. Some of them were rather magnificent, sporting thick manes as they perched proudly on tall cat trees. Others were slinky and thin, sliding like shadows through an obstacle course. Some were old and large and sleeping, and at least half a dozen kittens batted balls of yarn against the wall. Madeline was tempted. It looked like a petting zoo. Would it be okay to go in and just pet the cats for a few minutes? Maybe there was one that she needed to meet.

No, that was silly, Madeline scolded herself. Why in the world would she need to *meet* a cat? She shook the thought from her mind as she moved past the shop on her way to the liquor store.

OVER THE COURSE of the day, Jimmy had found homes for six cats, including Macy Gray, who'd become impatient with her kittens lately and would probably welcome the solitude. Mickey didn't seem terribly happy about the recent changes in residency, though. She'd been restless all afternoon but didn't want to play. Jimmy tried to pet and soothe her until at last she'd fallen asleep on the windowsill, where she still was now. Soon he'd be celebrating with his little family. He had a turkey waiting in the oven upstairs and he'd left his guitar by the door in anticipation of some after-dinner serenading.

Once upon a time, Jimmy had had two dreams. Not dreams in the literal sense, but dreams in the figurative sense. When he was just a kid, moving from foster home to foster home, he'd thought someday he wanted to own a place of his own. A business-type place, with living quarters attached. He'd checked that dream off the day he'd opened his store, and it had felt good. But there had been a second dream, too—a bit more far-fetched. Jimmy had wanted to be a magician.

Not a stage magician. More like a sorcerer. Someone who studied the lost arts and learned how to perform spells and then became the very best. Of course, that was one of those stupid dreams, the sort a kid had before he learned how the world worked, and as a black man growing up at the mercy of the foster care system, Jimmy had certainly learned how the world worked.

During his days as a runaway when he'd decided to escape the system, Jimmy had gotten into some fairly serious encounters with other folks who lived in the park where he'd camped out. Humans could be just as territorial as cats—no, worse—and one event stood out in his mind as a particularly close call with death. He'd been living in a tent at the edge of some hiking trails, eating canned food he'd picked up here and there, and steadily losing hope. Things had kept getting worse and worse, and Jimmy had started to think they would never get any better—that maybe he'd die out there in the woods, alone and homeless.

The day passed, twilight had arrived, and Jimmy was sitting at what should have been his campfire, trying to get the flame to catch, but the wind kept blowing it out. Over and over again, he'd start to get a little glow and *poof*—nothing. Jimmy swore to himself. He cursed and spit and then he stood up. To hell with it, he thought. To hell with *all* of it.

No sooner had he thought this than Jimmy heard the sound of a drunken group of men stumbling through the nearby woods. They were burping and hollering and generally making a ruckus. Jimmy felt himself go as still as a panther as fear itched through his body before being replaced shortly by rage. Why the hell did he feel like *he* had to be the one to hide out when it was them who were trespassing on what little bit of a home he'd managed to claim for himself?

Righteous anger had filled Jimmy's veins and he'd stomped over his attempts at a fire in the direction of the group. He opened his mouth to yell at those motherfuckers to *get the fuck off his land* and then out of nowhere he felt the command:

STOP. DON'T MOVE. DROP.

And because he decided to listen to that voice Jimmy had dropped flat to the ground just in time to feel a bullet graze the side of his neck as he fell. He lay there, breathing and bleeding, with his face buried in the dead leaves and brambles of the forest floor while the men fired more shots into the air where Jimmy's head had just been.

Jimmy didn't get up and face those men that night. If he had, he surely would have died. But after that, something new came over him; he felt he recovered a sense of direction and purpose. Step by step, Jimmy found his way out of the woods. He found a place in the city and started working his way up. Eventually, he managed to buy a place of his own, and rather than setting up as a traditional pet store, Jimmy used his shop to help cats who were down and out because if he didn't, well, then who the hell would?

Jimmy glanced at the *open* sign in the window. He really should turn it—it was unlikely anyone else would come in at this hour, especially in this weather. But first, turkey. He'd go upstairs, get it from the oven, and close up shop when he came back down.

CHAPTER NINETEEN

CLUTCHING THE PAPER bag of wine in one hand, Madeline exited the liquor store and began to make her way back to the corner on her return trip to the subway. She studied the route to Sam's parents' house on her phone. From here, she'd have to head back to the station and take the subway two more stops, then walk the rest of the way. It would be another twenty-five minutes before she could see the creature that had taken Sam's place. After that, no matter how things went, Madeline felt she'd be able to write her story's ending.

To her left, Madeline heard the sound of scratching on glass. In the window of *Jimmy's Used Cat Emporium*, a small orange kitten with a white star on its forehead was looking at her with prescient yellow eyes.

"Well, hello there," cooed Madeline, bending down to get a better look at the kitten as it raised its right paw to the glass and scratched again.

It mewed, and even outside in the cold snow Madeline's heart melted. The kitten stared right at her, holding eye contact and refusing to look away, and the longer Madeline looked into its bright round eyes the more familiar it seemed to be. Maybe it reminded her of a pet she'd had when she was young, but Madeline couldn't be sure. A strong urge rose in her to hold the kitten close—to nuzzle its nose, to pet it and feed it and brush it and adore it for as long as they both should live. But Madeline really didn't need a cat, nor were pets allowed in her apartment.

The sign on the door was still turned to *open* and Madeline decided a quick visit couldn't hurt anyone. Besides, she was late already and not exactly in a rush.

Shifting the paper bag under her left arm, Madeline pushed the open door. A bell tinkled overhead and she had to catch her balance as a few cats rushed against her feet, all begging for attention at once. Steadying her balance with the help of the door, Madeline looked around the shop. None of the cats were cooped up in cages; they were all wandering free. She went to the window and the kitten was still there, watching her with an expression that was somewhere between eager and wary.

"Hello," Madeline greeted it, extending her hand. Her bare fingertips poked out of her fingerless gloves and the kitten sniffed them tentatively, and then rubbed its cheek against her knuckles. "Oh, what a good little kitty," she cooed. "Is it okay if I hold you?" She rested the bottle of wine against the wall and reached for the kitten with both hands. It allowed itself be scooped up and Madeline cradled it lovingly against her chest.

"Oh." A deep voice from behind startled Madeline and she whirled around. A tall black man was holding a platter of sliced turkey, his eyes wide in apparent surprise. Madeline felt like an unwelcome intruder. The kitten in her arms began to claw and twist and Madeline was obliged to set it down on the carpeted floor. Once free, it sped over to the man and twisted around his ankle, rubbing its cheek against his boots.

"Oh, hi," said Madeline. "Sorry, I was just—"

"Saying hello to Mickey," he finished for her.

Madeline furrowed her brows in confusion. "Who?"

The man nodded at the kitten and Madeline understood. "Oh, yeah, sure, that's right. I was just saying hello to Mickey."

"She's a fine little kitten, isn't she?"

"Yeah! I mean, I guess."

"You're not gonna find any kitten smarter than this one, or more sassy, or discerning." The man's chest swelled as he praised the kitten. It was clearly one of his favorites.

"Is that right?"

"But very tolerant," he continued. "She never complains about my music."

Madeline nodded, unsure of what to add to the conversation. This was awkward, and growing more uncomfortable by the moment. Clearly, the man liked the cat a lot.

"In fact," he went on, "I could go on and on about Mickey. You know how they say most cats don't recognize faces in the mirror? Well, she does. She recognizes mine, and she recognizes hers, too. Now, what do you think of that? Do you think she could be a cat celebrity?"

"Well, I don't know."

The man laughed good-naturedly and bent to stroke the kitten's head. "I'm just kidding. Too much attention like that would go straight to her head. Isn't that right, little girl? Now, then, would you like some turkey?"

It took Madeline a minute to understand he wasn't talking to the cat, but to her. "Oh," she started, "Thanks, but I'm a vegetarian."

"Vegetarian!" he exclaimed. "Now, what in the heck do you eat on Thanksgiving if turkey's off the menu?"

Madeline smiled. This was not the first time she'd been asked that question. "I eat other food. Sometimes Tofurkey."

"To-whatsit? What in the world is that?"

"It's like tofu," said Madeline, and she could feel herself blushing, as if the food she ate was ridiculous. "Fake meat that's been filled with stuffing."

"Well, I'm afraid I don't have any of that. Do you eat other things? What about cheese and crackers? I was just about to have dinner, but the cats and I would love some company."

Madeline's blush deepened. It was getting too hot in here. She pulled off her hat. "I don't know. You see…"

"What about carrots? Ranch dressing?"

"Yeah, sure, I eat those things."

"Chocolate!" said the man with a spark of enthusiasm. "Now, tell me you eat chocolate?"

"Well, yes," admitted Madeline, smiling despite herself as she unzipped her coat. "I do eat chocolate."

"Don't move a muscle," he said. "I'll be back in a jiffy. I've got just the thing." He set the plate of steaming turkey on the counter beside a hungry-looking cat that started to nose into it immediately. Madeline hurried over, shooing the cat away so she could stand guard around the roasted bird until he returned. The kitten named Mickey remained in the place the man had stood. Eventually, she relaxed and began to lick her hind feet, carefully running her tongue into the crevices between each toe.

Recovered from her round of blushing, Madeline pulled off her coat and laid it on the counter beside the platter. She added her hat to the pile and then her scarf. "Well," said Madeline, presumably to the kitten. The man had spoken quite familiarly to it so she supposed she could, too. "It looks like I'm staying for dinner. Maybe that's just as well. Showing up this late to Sam's party would be pretty rude, wouldn't it? Still, if I can't see Sam, then how am I going to figure out what to write next about the ghost? I need to finish my story."

"The what?" the man asked as he reemerged from the back room.

"Nothing." Madeline cleared her throat as the blush crept back into her cheeks. She realized that perhaps confessing her innermost thoughts to a cat wasn't so normal after all.

"Well, that's good, because I thought I heard you say 'the ghost' and if there's one thing Thanksgiving doesn't need, it's any ghosts. Leave the ghosts for Halloween, and have them gone by Thanksgiving. That's what I say. Now, take a look at what I found. Is this all right?"

The man pushed aside the plate of turkey and presented a platter piled high with store-bought chocolate chip cookies, dozens of wrapped bonbons, a variety of neatly cut hard cheeses, carrots, and Ritz crackers. This would be more than sufficient to feed Madeline, and she graciously accepted a cracker and topped it with a cube of cheese.

"It's great," Madeline said by way of thanks, covering her mouth as she chewed. "This is so nice. You didn't have to—"

"Nonsense," interrupted the man, "but let's not stand around like barbarians. Let's be civilized. Have a seat. Pull up a chair. Grab that one in the corner." He pointed with an authoritative finger and Madeline retrieved a plush yellow chair, hauling it over to what was probably normally used as a display counter for goods. "And while you're over there," he called, "will you turn that sign on the door over? We are officially closed."

Madeline paused in her chair pulling and went to the door. She hesitated a second before flipping the *open* sign to *closed* because this seemed exactly like a set-up for some kind of murder mystery scenario—a woman disappears on Thanksgiving and her body is never found because it was fed in tiny little bits to dozens of hungry cats. But, if this man were really bad, Madeline was sure she'd get a feeling. Her intuition had never failed her before.

"Wonderful." The man gave Madeline a pleased smile

as they took their seats on opposite sides of the counter. "Except wait, something's missing. Drinks! I knew I was forgetting something. I should have gone and picked up a bottle of wine, but oh well, dinner's ready, so we'll have to make do with tap water. Do you take ice in yours?" he asked, standing up once more.

"No," said Madeline, shaking her head. Her blush was starting again, and she shouldn't, it was weird, but she offered anyway. "No ice, but I actually have some wine right here," she said, rising to fetch the bottle from where she'd left the paper bag against the wall. As she revealed it, the grin on the man's face widened further.

"How's that!" he remarked with obvious satisfaction. "Don't you ever let anyone tell you there's no such thing as magic. I'll be back in a flash, but go ahead and get started—don't wait for me."

Madeline set the wine on the counter and took her seat, though she immediately had to get up again to pull excited cats off the table.

The man returned, carrying glasses full of water, two wine glasses, and a bowl full of chopped turkey that, after depositing the glasses on the counter, he set down on the floor to satisfy the cats. Madeline had no idea how he managed it all without spilling a drop.

"Now," the man said, dropping into his seat, his eyes twinkling with a satisfied sort of look that suggested all was well in the world. "Let's have some of that wine and you can tell me all about yourself, okay?"

"Um," Madeline stuttered, feeling her anxious blush returning. This time, she chose to ignore it. "Okay, sure, why not. My name is Madeline. What's yours?"

The man slapped a hand against his knee. "Oh, goodness," he laughed. "I'm sorry. I thought you already knew. I'm Jimmy, and this is my *Used Cat Emporium*."

CHAPTER TWENTY

PETER COULDN'T UNDERSTAND how Sam could sit there and not even look at him—at any of them. It was like she was pretending none of them existed. She was so self-satisfied, and she didn't give a damn. But he loved her. Even after all this, Peter loved her more than life.

Sam's family was big on board games. They had an entire cupboard full of them, and after everyone had eaten, dessert was delayed in favor of a game. It was another activity Peter had only grudgingly participated in during visits with Sam's family, always feeling like he was left hanging on the edges of the fun—a spectator to a lifetime's worth of shared inside jokes. He always lost, too.

For better or worse, Sam was also now a spectator. Bianca wanted to include her in the game—a slapstick one called Apples to Apples—but Sam just stared at the cards in front of her blankly, though she'd played the game many times before. She picked up a card and licked it.

"I'll talk her through it," Peter volunteered. He scooted his chair closer to Sam's and took the card before she could bite it or stuff it in her mouth. He wanted to help her. He wanted to be useful. He picked up the cards that were meant to be hers and held them up where she could see them.

They made it through two rounds of the game before Sam had enough. She knocked the cards out of Peter's hand and grabbed his wrist roughly beneath the table, twisting it.

"*I'm hungry*," she hissed in his ear.

"You can't be," he mumbled. Peter felt everyone's eyes on him and he tried to gain control. He put his hand on Sam's where it grabbed at his wrist, and then he stood, pulling her up with him and trying to make it look as smooth as possible. "Maybe she needs a change of scenery," Peter suggested weakly. "I'll take her on a little walk. Some fresh air might help."

He felt everyone watching them as he exited the room with Sam in tow. He'd never have been able to handle her like this back when she was herself. She'd have fought him more violently—kicked him in the shin, kneed him in the groin, bit him, no holds barred. Since the accident, her resistance had vanished. In fact, it felt more like she was the one leading him.

This suspicion was reinforced when they arrived at the front door and Sam didn't stop for their coats.

"Come on, you have to put your coat on," Peter said, struggling against Sam as she groped for the door. Finally, he managed to pull her coat on. The coat was quickly becoming too small for Sam's belly, and trying to stuff her into it was like wrestling a naughty child into a piece of clothing they'd long outgrown. There was no warning of this type of behavior from the doctors, no reason for her to be so stubborn, so resistant, and so goddamn hungry all the time. "What the hell's gotten into you, anyway?" Peter growled under his breath. He hadn't been alone with Sam, truly alone, for over a year. They'd lived separately in the six months before their divorce, and in the hospital he'd spoken to her frankly though there had almost always been doctors and nurses around to listen to their interactions. Peter was getting fed up. He needed to get through to Sam. He was changing his life—he was doing it for her—but things couldn't go on like this.

"Come on," he said, jerking the door open. Sam led the way out, yanking him along behind her. A faint memory came back to Peter of old lovers' spats when Sam would overreact to silly things and they'd hash it out and get physical and end up in bed, each of them struggling against the other until all the tension was gone and everything was forgiven. It gave Peter a faint hard on, which persevered despite the cold as they strode frantically for a couple of blocks, elbows linked and not speaking. Peter couldn't remember how they'd gotten like this—whether she'd taken his arm or he'd taken hers—but they crunched arm in arm through the thin layer of fresh snow that was still falling, bound together in the shared silence of body heat and frustration and discontent.

At last, they paused at a dark corner beneath a burnt out streetlamp and Peter felt a change come over Sam. Her arm against his went softer, like she'd released a long-held breath. Peter paused. He unlinked his arm from Sam's and turned her to face him.

"Sammy, talk to me. Please. If you're in there, tell me what's going on with you. Tell me why you're doing this. Are you angry? I know I was shit to you, and if you're angry, I deserve it. But I'm different now. I'm better. I've changed—I *swear* I've changed. It may have taken losing you to do it, but I'm not the man I used to be. I'm never going back to how I was before. Not ever. Sam, I can't."

He could hear emotion making his voice crack and he hoped it would break through her stonewalled silence. He was telling the truth. For once in his life, he knew it was the whole truth he was telling her.

"It's the truth, Sammy," Peter insisted, his voice rising with conviction.

Sam took a breath. She was about to answer him. He could feel it. He waited. He tried not to hope too much, but he was devastated. He needed her.

"You need me?" Sam asked softly, as if she had read his mind. Peter couldn't even marvel at the coincidence.

"Yes," he said simply. "Yes. I need you."

"I need something, too."

"What is it? I'll give you anything." Suddenly, Peter was desperate—desperate to please Sam, to prove himself to her.

"More life," Sam said, and she moved into him, pushing forward until his back made contact with the hard pole at his back. "I need more life. Give me your life." Her hands reached up to his neck and her icy fingers closed around his throat. These weren't Sam's fingers, not really, but they were close as he was ever going to get. Peter closed his eyes. He could have pushed her away, but he took one deep breath in and held it, held it like it was all the love he had left to give, and he let her take him.

THE GHOST TOOK of Peter's body, his breath, and his soul. It choked the love out, and then the fear, too. At the last moment, Peter opened his eyes in terror and the ghost felt almost sorry, but it pushed through. When it was over Peter was as still and peaceful as a baby, and coursing through the ghost was the vigor of fresh life. It was warm, as the ghost had known it would be, and the ghost's stomach unclenched, the endless pain finally receding. Tears rolled down its cheeks, a sensation the ghost hadn't experienced for...it didn't know how long.

The ghost was panting, invigorated, but the struggle was over. Now, the ghost could have a *real* meal. It knelt down beside where Peter's body had slumped to the ground. His eyes were open, blind and unseeing.

The ghost would start with those. Peter wouldn't mind.

It was the part of the human that should have been the most easily pluckable, but the ghost's new fingers were not the right tools. They were too thick. It should use a spoon, but it had none.

The ghost felt in its pockets for the butter knife it had stolen from the dinner table, just in case. It was a bit messy, but after some work, it did the job, cutting deep around the sphere of the eyeball and popping it out from the socket. The ghost swallowed one eye and then the other, both trailing long red strings of connective tissue that slithered down the ghost's throat as it consumed them. As Peter's eyes slid down the ghost's throat, the image of a woman's smiling face rose in its mind.

"Mommy," the ghost felt like saying to the face, but it wasn't Bianca's face. Perhaps it was another mother. Peter's mother. The ghost assumed all humans had one, it had no reason not to assume such a thing. An unfamiliar emotion overcame the ghost and it collapsed into the snow. In its vision, the woman's eyes were full of something shimmery—the same precious light it had often seen in Bianca's—and the ghost felt like its heart had burst open. What it had seen through Peter's eyes was sour to the ghost, toxic and inedible.

The ghost vomited large globs that included eyes and unchewed cheese and turkey and mashed potatoes. It wiped its mouth with the back of its hand. The ghost spat into the snow, trying to get it all out, but no matter how much it cast out of itself the feeling of distress lingered.

What was it the ghost had felt? Unbidden tears spilled down the ghost's cheeks as it looked at Peter: eyeless, lifeless, motherless. Gone. It would have to find another human to eat, something to clear the bitter aftertaste of broken-hearted longing.

The ghost dusted itself off, feeling strange. It wasn't

exactly hungry anymore, but in need of comfort. Peter's life energy was sad. It made the ghost tremble and weep without reason, and it found this emotion even more disturbing than the constant hunger.

Perhaps someone younger, someone fresher, might have a better aftertaste.

CHAPTER TWENTY-ONE

When Peter woke he saw his body lying in the snow underneath the burnt out streetlight. But that wasn't right. He must still be asleep.

Come on, Peter. Wake up, he tried thinking to himself, but the dream-scene persisted. He recognized the shape of a woman. It looked like it might have been Sam, but it was hard to tell in the darkness.

As Peter's eyes adjusted he saw that it was Sam, and she was crouched down over his body, doing something to his face—to his eyes. Peter drew closer, wanting to let her know that the body wasn't really his because he was here behind her, but as he came closer he noticed something strange. Sam's body was shimmering, and he could see through her skin.

There was something wrong with the person in front of him. On second inspection, Peter saw that the woman he had thought was Sam wasn't Sam at all. It was her body, but not *her*.

"Sam?" he said, and as if the sound of his voice had struck her, she fell backward, down into the snow. It wasn't a person. It was a *thing*—a thing that was somehow inside Sam's body and her body wasn't fitting it right. Her eyes looked upward, wide and staring, and Peter had a glimpse of a face wavering behind Sam's face. The face belonged to an imposter, a creature with bulging black eyes and a pinhole mouth. Peter realized with horror what had happened to him.

Sam had killed him, only it hadn't been Sam. It had been that *thing* inside of her—whatever had taken residence in Sam's body after she had died in that car accident, because, Peter realized now, that was what had happened. That thing—that hungry thing—had never been Sam. She had never woken up.

"No, no, no," Peter cried aloud, trying to un-see it. "This can't be real. It can't." And yet the memory of what had happened was coming back to him. They had left the house together, he and the Sam-thing. They had walked to the streetlight. He's offered to give himself to her, and she'd closed her hands around his neck

Peter had taken in one last breath, and then—

"What is this? What am I?" On one hand, Peter was terrified, but on the other, he was more confused than he'd ever been. "Is this heaven or hell? Am I a ghost? And what the fuck? What. The. FUCK."

He had just seen what Sam—not Sam—had done to his eyes.

Peter felt himself filling with rage, a more energetic state than confusion. Whatever this thing was—whatever it had done to him—it was disgusting. It was evil. He wanted revenge.

After everything he'd done, everything he'd worked so

hard to do for himself—for Sam—this is what his life had fucking come to: dead in the street on Thanksgiving and a ghost? A fucking ghost? It couldn't be real.

But it was.

"Fucking shit!" Peter cursed, grappling with the reality of it.

Maybe it was all a dream and he just needed to wake the fuck up.

"Come on, Peter. Try and remember. What were you doing? Did you fall asleep somewhere?"

He must have been back in his apartment, passed out drunk again on the couch, watching television. No, he had quit drinking. He was sure of it. But asleep on the couch, that had to be it. Yes, without a doubt, real life had left off last night. He was just having a nightmare, caused by stress over Thanksgiving. Sam wasn't some demon creature. This was a bad dream, a sign he shouldn't go to the party. When he woke up he would listen. He'd phone Bianca and apologize, and he'd see Sam some other time.

"I'm just dreaming," Peter tried to convince himself. "This is a dream, and I'll prove it. If it's a dream, I can do anything. I can fly." He concentrated, and almost instantly energy surged upward from the bottoms of his feet, pushing him into the air.

Peter laughed victoriously. He raised his arms high and congratulated his own clever thinking. "What did I tell you, Peter old boy? Totally dreaming!" But now that

Peter was up high, he was unsure where to go. The city stretched out below him, picturesque and startlingly clear. He must have night vision. This dream was awesome. Where should he go? What should he do?

He could go to a nightclub, see some dancers. Maybe catch a movie. No, that was too mundane. *Come on, Peter*, he chastised himself, *if you could do anything...*

He'd go and see Sam.

Sam. The thought triggered something he wasn't ready to think about just yet.

Far below, in the street, he could make out Sam's figure—or at least the figure of the thing that he had thought was Sam. She'd left the dark area under the burnt out streetlamp and was moving back in the direction of the house. Memories of the night's earlier events came back to him, forcing their way through his dream and into reality. Sam's family was there—her parents, her brother, her sister-in-law, and her little nieces. So if—just supposing—that creature really wasn't Sam...and if this wasn't a dream...and if she'd done to him what he thought she'd done...

"Okay, Peter, it's time to man up," Peter told himself. He swooped back down to the street, following closely behind Sam.

"Who are you?" Peter called, wondering if she could hear him. Either she couldn't or she was ignoring him. It was hard to tell. "*What* are you?" he tried again, more forcefully this time. He observed her closely, studying her shimmering quality. It was as if some creature was squeezed into Sam's flesh, moving her body like an ill-fitting flesh costume. If that were the case, where the hell was Sam? Had she actually died in the accident, or had this thing done something more nefarious to her—pushed her out of her body somehow while she'd been unconscious? Peter didn't have the faintest idea how ghosts or demons or little pinhole-mouthed creatures stole human bodies. He hadn't even known they'd existed at all until just now—assuming he wasn't dreaming, of course.

Peter closed the distance that separated him and the Sam-thing, hovering just behind her shoulder as he evaluated the ethereal texture of her body. He took a breath. Could he move inside her body, too? And more to the point, should he? Wouldn't it be invasive, or disgusting, or weird?

I am not really a ghost. This is just a weird dream, Peter reassured himself, and he reached out one dream hand.

There was a light pressure, but then his hand dipped straight through Sam's shimmery skin. It was nasty, or cool. Exciting. He could go...

Inside her.

He gulped.

Peter shivered with something that might have been erotic pleasure. It had been so long—so fucking, *fucking* long—and how he ached for her!

Before Peter could chicken out, he stepped in entirely,

and it wasn't at all difficult, just a faint resistance and then entry. He was larger than her, and he stuck out awkwardly at the front and sides, but around him, and through him, was Sam's body, moving as the other thing inside her propelled itself forward. He tried to pace her, to remain inside.

He didn't really want to pontificate on why he was doing this. Some kind of cathartic bullshit, probably. Another one of his invasions into Sam's life. Or, not her life, as it would seem. His either, for that matter.

Someone younger, someone fresher... Someone small... A little girl...

What was that? What was he hearing? Was it the thing inside Sam?

Peter's dead now... Gone...

"No, I'm not!" Peter shouted defiantly.

Peter went still and let Sam walk out of him, having found that experiment to be less satisfying than he had desired. What had the Sam-thing meant by someone small? Why was it talking about a little—

Oh.

Peter had a rush of understanding, and it was not good.

Sam—or whatever she was now—had arrived outside of the house and was stepping onto the path that led to the stairs to the front door. If he were going to warn anyone, he'd have to do so fast.

CHAPTER TWENTY-TWO

ROSA WAS STILL hungry. The food had been okay. She liked the mashed potatoes, piled high with a tiny bit of gravy in a puddle on top. She'd had at least six bites of corn and some carrots, but despite her grandma's earlier promise, she hadn't had any cookies—and she really, really wanted pie.

"Stop it," Rosa reprimanded Diane. Her little sister was grabbing at her arm, trying to pull her away to go play their game of fairies and firemen. The game had been Rosa's idea. The fairies started fires and the firemen put them out. Sometimes the fairies caused floods and the firemen had to evaporate them, and sometimes they fell in love and tried to make babies, but the firemen were stupid, and the fairies were smart, so they fought a lot. Rosa had tired of playing that game. She wanted to go do something else. She wanted Auntie Sam to read her a book. "I said, stop!" Rosa cried, pushing away her little sister. "Mom," she cried, "Didi won't stop grabbing me!"

Annoyance shadowed Carly's face as she turned away from the card game she was playing with the other adults and faced her daughters reprovingly. She got less patient and a little mean whenever she drank wine, and Rosa knew what was coming.

"Diane Simmons," her mother snapped, "keep your hands to yourself."

Throwing her arms across her chest, Diane pouted. She kicked the chair legs with her feet and rocked back and forth, making a moaning sound. She was only a few years younger than Rosa, but she was such a baby.

"Go find something else to do," Rosa said, slipping down off the chair. She didn't want to play, but she also didn't want Diane to get too mad and throw a fit, so she tried to be helpful. "Help Mom with the card game. If you're good, maybe she'll give you pie," she added in a whisper.

Diane looked at her hopefully. Rosa loved having big sister power. She could talk Diane into anything.

"That's right," she said, nodding encouragingly as she grew more confident in her lie. "If you're really good and you watch Mom play cards, she'll give you pie. But you have to be *very* good, okay? That means no following me and no kicking the chair—and no crying. Okay?"

Diane pressed her lips together and nodded trustingly.

"Good." Rosa patted the top of Diane's head and kissed it for good measure, inhaling the sweet smell of her powdery little sister.

"What a cutie," she heard her grandpa say, and Rosa smiled to herself as she concluded her performance with a sneaky exit.

"Not so fast." Rosa's mom caught her by the wrist. She was jerked to an indelicate stop. "Just where do you think you're going?"

"To get a book. Auntie Sam's been reading *Charlotte's Web* to me."

"Oh, yes. That's right." Her mother's face softened, and she looked down at Rosa with most of her attention. "You were reading that together, weren't you? I had forgotten. But I think Auntie Sam is busy right now, with Unc—with Peter. And anyway, it wouldn't be very nice to read without Diane, would it?"

"But she fell asleep last time," Rosa whined, trying to keep her voice down so Diane wouldn't hear. "And she's too little. She won't remember."

"Well..." Her mom's attention was called away by the sound of laughter from the other adults. "What's the word? Grotesque? Oh, I've got a good one..." She released Rosa's wrist, and Rosa rubbed it, feeling free, but her mom looked at her again before she could get away. Rosa made her eyes wide and innocent. She couldn't blink, she couldn't blink.

"You can go and get the book," her mom agreed at last with a stern look, "but I don't know when Auntie Sam is coming back. And don't make a mess!" she added as Rosa slipped out and made her way to the guest room, where Grandma kept children's books for when she and her sister visited.

It was rare for Rosa to have alone time and she relished it. This whole big house was hers. The adults were busy, and she was going to get a book and read a whole page by herself. Then, when Auntie Sam came back, she'd impress her by showing off what she'd done. Auntie Sam would make a big fuss. She'd cuddle her and tell her how smart she was and then Rosa would ask her to read more things, bigger and harder words, and Rosa would do it, and Auntie Sam would be so proud she'd make all the adults be quiet and listen to Rosa read. Auntie Sam loved Rosa the best, and Rosa loved Auntie Sam the best, too… at least she did when Auntie Sam wasn't being weird like she was since she'd come home from the hospital.

Rosa reached up and caught hold of the doorknob to the guest room, then twisted and pushed the door open wide. She felt up high for the light switch and fumbled around until she caught it. The lights were bright when she flicked them on and they hurt her eyes a little. Rosa went over to the bookcase and knelt down, running her finger over each title as she paused to consider it. She knew the one she was looking for had two words, one long and one short. It was a thick book with a hardcover. There was a pig on the front, and a spider—Wilbur and Charlotte.

After running her finger over about a bazillion books Rosa determined the one she was looking for was not there, and she sat down heavily on the floor in disappointment. Now she wasn't going to be able to read anything to impress Auntie Sam *or* find out what had happened to Wilbur and Charlotte. It had been a long time since she and Auntie Sam had read together—since before the accident—and her memory of the story was fading. Charlotte was trying to help Wilbur, to save him. He was a… What was it, a fantastic pig? Charlotte had made him into that to save his life.

Rosa leaned her head back against the bookcase. This was no fun. What was the use of having the whole house to herself if she couldn't have fun?

She was still staring at the stark whiteness of the ceiling and the interesting patterns created by cracks in the drywall when the lights above her head flickered. Rosa straightened up and looked around, suddenly alert. If the lights were flickering, it could be nothing—maybe a bulb dying, that's what her dad would say—or it might be something scary. She'd seen on one of her mother's TV shows that sometimes ghosts do things like make the lights go funny when they were trying to get your attention.

"Hello?" Rosa whispered in a barely audible voice, and then she listened really hard, but there wasn't any response. The little girl was suddenly very lonely in the big house all by herself.

The lights flickered again and Rosa decided it was something scary after all.

If it was a ghost, how did she talk to it? Rosa tried to remember based on the scary movies she'd seen her parents watching when she'd snuck out of bed. She didn't think ghosts had voices, but she was pretty sure they could move stuff around.

"If you are a ghost," she whispered in a voice a little

louder and a bit more brave, "pick up a book from the shelf and move it in the air."

She turned to stare at the bookshelf, then held her breath and waited. Was that a wiggle? No. Nothing happened. It must not be a ghost after all, just a boring dying light bulb.

Rosa slumped back down, but then the lights started flickering wildly, off and on and off and on and off and on and off and on.

Rosa leaped to her feet. "Stop! It's not funny!"

But the lights kept on flickering. Something twisted in Rosa's belly, and she ran from the room without closing the door behind her.

Mom! She was about to shout, but the word caught in her throat because there was someone standing at the end of the hallway staring at her. She stopped.

It took a moment, but then Rosa recognized the shape of her aunt. "Auntie Sam?" she called, her voice only quivering a little. Auntie Sam was staring at her and smiling, but her face didn't look right. Actually, the person at the other end of the hall didn't look like her Auntie Sam at all. It was her body but the face was different, like it belonged to a stranger.

"Hello, little girl," Auntie Sam said like she didn't even know Rosa's name.

"What do you want?" Rosa demanded.

"Do you like pie?"

For the first time, Rosa noticed a whole pie in Auntie

Sam's hands. She must have gotten some on her shirt, because the front of her chest was stained with red and it looked like she had some on the back of her hand, too.

"What kind is it?" said Rosa, tempted by the potential of dessert. She thought about the flavors that were red. "Cherry?"

"I like pie," said Auntie Sam, "and I like you."

"Okay," Rosa said, but the word came out wobbly because even though she did like Auntie Sam—she *loved* Auntie Sam—she did not like the way Auntie Sam was acting right now. It was even scarier than the ghost flickering lights in the bedroom with the books.

"One fish, two fish, red fish, blue. I like pie, and I like you," Auntie Sam sang the words so that they sounded like a silly song, and Rosa cracked a smile in spite of herself. That sounded more like the Auntie Sam she remembered, making storybook rhymes to get her to laugh.

"I like pie," volunteered Rosa, "but not green eggs and ham."

"Then 'Let's eat pie' said Sam I Am." Auntie Sam grinned but it wasn't a happy grin. It was too big, and it didn't fit her face like her usual smile. It reminded Rosa of the Grinch and the way he smiled before ruining all the Whos Christmases in the holiday special.

Rosa hesitated, but then chastised herself for being silly. There were no such things as ghosts or Grinches. They were just make-believe. Auntie Sam was real, and she was holding a great big cherry pie just for her.

"Come here," called Auntie Sam, balancing the pie on one hand and holding out the other—the one without the red stuff on it—to Rosa. "Let's have a little treat. Just you and me."

"Like on my birthday?" Rosa asked, remembering another time when she and her aunt had snuck a dessert for themselves.

Auntie Sam nodded, the Grinchy grin never leaving her face. "Yes. Exactly like that."

BIANCA WAS TRYING to play a game with her family like nothing was wrong, even though her entire life was falling apart around her. Sam was a mess. She hated to say it—to even think it—but it was true, she had to admit it. She'd never seen her daughter like this, not even when things had been at their worst during her divorce from Peter. Having her at home, outside of the insulating bubble of the hospital, made the truth so much more obvious. Bianca couldn't even blame it on the accident or the drugs the doctors had given Sam anymore.

And now Peter had taken her outside, out of her sight. What were they doing out there, anyway? Fighting? *Kissing?* He'd better not lay a hand on her. Bianca would cut them both off. Thank God Sam had never gotten pregnant when she'd been married to that man. Not that Bianca didn't want another grandchild—oh, she did, and Sam's would be beautiful—but then again, Peter's

wouldn't be. If you took beautiful and combined it with…
but no, that was too harsh. Peter hadn't always been as he
was now. Once, Sam had loved him.

Bianca shivered. The wine was getting to her. She'd
lost count of how many drinks she'd had during this party
she wished she hadn't thrown. It was never-ending—*life*
was never-ending. Sam was eating her out of house and
home, *literally*. Never had a cliché that was so absurd-
ly, obviously hyperbolic been so actually true. And now
she was mingling outside, in her vulnerable state, with the
man who'd stolen the best years of her life.

"I'll just go and check on them out there," Bianca said,
rising abruptly from her chair and placing her cards down
on the table without even bothering to turn them over.
She went through the kitchen toward the front windows.
It would be too motherly to go out after them, and Sam,
even if she was different, was not a child, but it was so
dark outside. Bianca couldn't see a thing—just rows of
street lamps, and a few blocks down, one that was out.

She looked at the corner that should have been lit. She
hadn't noticed before the light was out, but supposed it
must have been for a while. She hoped they hadn't gone
far. She hoped Peter was behaving himself.

Peter. She had such mixed feeling about that man. On
one hand, he was a no-good asshole, failure, drunk. And
on the other…

The other hand came up empty. It always did, no matter how she tried to weigh it out.

Bianca sighed. The wine was giving her a headache. She should bring out the pie and be a good hostess to the rest of her family.

Turning, she noticed one of the pies was missing. In the place where it had been, a faint string of crumbs had been arranged into a name.

Rosa, it read.

Bianca knew then it hadn't just been motherly instinct gone awry, or an effect of too much wine. Something was definitely wrong.

CHAPTER TWENTY-THREE

THE KITTEN STAYED close while Madeline and Jimmy feasted, and Madeline kept one eye on her, following her feline movements as she stalked around the room. Half the time it seemed like the kitten's attention was on Jimmy in a distinctly non-catlike, almost human way, and the other half of the time she was distracted by bits of fluff and the activities of the other cats. In any case, she didn't seem to be paying much attention at all to Madeline, and Madeline could feel herself growing restless as well as becoming slightly irritated at being ignored—by a cat. The feeling was oddly familiar.

"Do you believe people go somewhere after they die?" Madeline wondered out loud during a pause in the conversation. It was a weird question, but Jimmy didn't seem to notice.

"Go somewhere?" he asked, giving her an amused little smile. "You mean like Heaven?"

"Kind of, yeah. Or somewhere else. Another life, maybe."

"It's funny you should ask," said Jimmy, resting his glass at his side and looking away. He seemed to be turning something over in his mind, and then, decided, he fixed his eyes on Madeline. "Do you want to hear a funny story?"

Before Madeline could say anything, Jimmy launched into a long and extravagant speech.

JIMMY HAD GROWN up in a string of foster homes. The fourth one had been the best on a list of bad experiences. At that house, he'd had three foster brothers and two foster sisters, but none of them had gotten along with him. They'd all been biologically related, and white, and his foster mother—her name was Mary—had favored them, giving them bigger portions and spending time with them, asking them how their days went and taking them on picnics, stuff like that. Jimmy had been left to fend for himself, taking food the others were given when they weren't looking, punching them in the noses if it came to it, but generally doing his best to keep to himself. Stu, his foster dad, had beaten him a couple of times for insubordination, though Jimmy didn't recall ever actually being insubordinate. Then, maybe because Mary was harboring some kind of guilt in her soul for the way they'd mistreated him, on his tenth birthday she took him to get a cat.

Decades later, Jimmy could still remember that day clearly. They'd gone to the pound and asked if there were any cats that had been picked up recently and not claimed. The boy who worked there—he was hardly more than a teenager—had gone into the back and returned a moment later with a shorthaired, gray-striped, orange-eyed tom.

The boy had carried the cat under its arms, so the legs were all spread out and Jimmy could see the patches of hair missing from the belly, as well as one long scar.

The cat, like Jimmy, was a fighter.

Jimmy named the cat Elvis before he was set down on the counter. Elvis didn't meow or hiss, but he had given Jimmy a look like steel. It was a *You don't fuck with me, I don't fuck with you* sort of look. Jimmy recognized it because he used it a lot himself.

They took Elvis home and because Jimmy knew to leave him alone, he quickly became Elvis' favorite. The other kids would harass Elvis and try to pet him or grab him while Jimmy would retreat to the bed in his corner of the room. After a while, Elvis would follow him and sit at the foot of Jimmy's bed. He never looked at Jimmy directly when he was nearby, but Jimmy knew Elvis was paying attention to him. He could feel it.

Jimmy developed a habit of saving a scrap of meat from dinner in his napkin for Elvis. He'd tuck it in his pocket and wait until they were excused from the table, and then when the other kids were either not around or asleep and couldn't tattle, he'd deliver the treat. Elvis would appear from wherever he'd been all day and take the morsel straight from Jimmy's fingers. No matter where Elvis was—out back around by the flowerbeds or down the block chasing birds in the park—Jimmy could trust that Elvis would slink in and sidle his way up to Jimmy, ready for whatever it was Jimmy could offer him that day.

What Jimmy had with Elvis felt like a real friendship, the kind two true fighters could manage. Elvis was the only friend Jimmy had. He'd had to change schools and never got to see his old pals anymore, and he sure as hell didn't get along with the friends of the other kids in the family. They'd harass Jimmy and treat him like dirt, try and get him to do stuff for them, call him stupid and a bastard. Jimmy did his best to ignore it, and if the house were full of idiots, Jimmy would go to the park and shoot some hoop. If the basketball were flat, which it often was, he'd sit on the merry-go-round, not going around and around, but just leaning back and looking up at the sky, waiting for the purpose of life to drop down on him.

When he'd gone home after one such day, his foster parents had been fighting. They didn't fight as much as some of his other foster parents had, but they still had their rows. Jimmy had gone to his room, too depressed to even read a comic book. A week later Elvis had gotten sick.

"He's all right, probably just tired," Mary said when Jimmy pointed out how Elvis was sitting in the corner, not in one of his usual places, and not moving.

"I don't think so," Jimmy said in a knowing sort of way. "I think something's wrong."

Mary hadn't listened. A month later the whole lot of them left on a big family vacation and left Jimmy behind to watch the house. Jimmy and Elvis had the place to themselves for a week and it should have been fun—a week of freedom—but Jimmy spent it worrying himself sick over Elvis's worsening health. He tried giving him leftover bits of chicken from the fridge, but the cat wouldn't chew, only look at him sadly. Elvis started making eye contact and Jimmy returned it. It was like the cat knew he didn't have much time left, and his pride had left him and he was searching for something in Jimmy's eyes.

On the fourth day, when the meat was gone and Jimmy was going to have to move on to Spam and packages of ramen noodles, Jimmy couldn't find Elvis in the house. He was in a full-blown panic by the time he finally found the cat in the park, near the swings. He had seen the way Elvis was lying in the gravel, how there was an unnatural stillness about him, and he rushed over. Elvis was still breathing, but barely.

Jimmy sat down on the ground next to Elvis, and when the cat found his eyes, Jimmy started to talk. "I wish I knew what to tell you," Jimmy said, stroking Elvis' head before resting his hand on his side. The cat's breathing was shallow, but Jimmy could feel him purring—a faint purr that might have been more out of pain than pleasure, more need than contentment. "I don't know if there's any point to any of this either, friend. We live, we suffer, and we die. We don't get much say in how any of it goes, but if I'll go anywhere after all of this is over, then I'll tell you what: you will, too."

Moments later he felt Elvis go still. No dramatic yowling, no twitching, no licks of farewell, just a quiet passing, and the purring beneath his hand—the faint tremble—stopped. Jimmy would never admit to having cried, but he had. He'd held Elvis, felt his soft, still-warm body, and he hadn't wanted to let him go. It was hard to bury a friend, and harder to think he hadn't been able to comfort him. But sometimes there wasn't any comfort.

Sometimes things just hurt.

That was when Jimmy had made his rule about not getting attached to any cats. But, from that point on, Jimmy made it his habit to observe them, especially the strays. Eventually, he felt the miracle of each of them, of their limited time on earth. He named them sometimes, and watched as they fought over territory, listened to their voices in the night, and kept a careful distance. He found himself developing an intuitive sense of cats and their shadowy, elusive spirits. Of all the things he watched, the birth of a new litter of kittens was what touched him the most, particularly when the littlest of the litter was pushed aside and left to fend on its own. Jimmy saw himself in those kittens—abandoned, orphaned, cast out. Everyone needed a home, he decided, and even though Jimmy couldn't provide much, he did what he could.

He'd done his best over the years to show everyone that even used cats could have a second life if given a chance.

WHEN JIMMY HAD finished his story, Madeline wasn't sure

what to say. She tried, "So, what you're saying is you're good at understanding cats?"

"Now, just a second," said Jimmy, raising one finger in the air. "Here comes the relevant bit."

Madeline lifted an eyebrow, wondering what could be coming next after all that.

"If I take a cat and hold her—for instance, little Mickey here—"

The kitten had been hanging close by while Madeline and Jimmy chatted, and Jimmy reached down now and scooped her up from the floor where she'd been watching them with half-lidded eyes.

"I can get an impression of what happened to them in their past life. I mean, before they came to my store. It's part of what helps me rehabilitate them. By figuring out what went wrong in their life before they got to me, I can get them what they need, whether that's time alone, or mothering, or medical care. Now, sometimes the information I get from these sessions is really detailed. In a few cases—and you might be impressed by this," he pointed emphatically at Madeline, "I've been able to *verify* information by tracking down a cat's previous owners and it's turned out to be correct." He paused to let that sink in and Madeline tried to look impressed. Jimmy set Mickey back down on the floor and the kitten scurried away while he rubbed his hands together, shrugging. "But anyhow, whatever you want to call that ability, and whether you even want to believe it or not, it's helped *me* to help *them*."

"Cool," said Madeline, still not knowing how this answered her original question about life after death. It had been so long, he'd probably forgotten she'd asked.

Jimmy looked at her sadly. "I must sound crazy to you."

"Well no, not exactly. It's just… never mind."

"Something bothering you? Why is it that you're out here alone on Thanksgiving, anyhow?"

"Because…" Madeline started, but she didn't know what to say. Because she was avoiding going to visit a woman who'd become someone unrecognizable? Because she was trying to get inspiration to finish a story about a hungry ghost consuming everything she once loved and was worried it was coming true? Because she was indecisive and looking for the world to give her the answers—but all she'd managed to do was find her way to a pet store where she'd been forced to listen to a story that didn't make any sense?

Mickey sniffed at Madeline's leg and Jimmy's eyes followed the cat.

"You look like you could use a friend. She can sense that."

Madeline reached down to Mickey but as she brought her hand close to the kitten's face, Mickey pivoted and raced back to Jimmy. It was irrational, but Madeline felt hurt and experienced a flash of anger. What was it about this kitten? Every time Madeline tried to pet it, it seemed interested and then shied away. Who did that remind her of?

"Could you do your thing with Mickey and get information about her past?" Madeline asked. She couldn't believe herself for asking something so ridiculous—clearly the wine was getting to her head.

Jimmy chuckled. "Mickey? I've had her since she was born, and she's only a few months old, so I doubt it..." Jimmy trailed off, but then seeing Madeline's expression, appeared to change his mind. "But why not, as a little experiment? I can try it and see what I can pick up on. Heck, it could be interesting."

He reached down and picked up the kitten. She struggled a little like she didn't want to be inspected, but Jimmy soothed her with his voice. "It's okay, don't be frightened. We're just going to have a little chat. Come this way," he instructed Madeline, standing up and setting off toward the back of the store. "If we want to do this properly, we'll need privacy. We don't need a bunch of other cats interfering in our business."

Madeline took one last, big gulp of her wine, set her glass down, and followed Jimmy through a door in the back where she found herself in a brightly lit hallway that glistened with fluorescent light. There were two doors, one directly in front of them and one down the hall to the right. Jimmy opened the first and Madeline followed him through, closing the door behind them.

The room was small and empty. With the door closed wall-to-wall and floor-to-ceiling carpeting muffled any sound. It was cozy, but in a strange way. Madeline probably should have been a little more uncomfortable than she was, but the wine coupled with a general feeling of fatigue made her willing to accept just about anything. Jimmy was a little odd, sure, but he felt safe.

"Okay," said Jimmy. "Come on, have a seat."

Jimmy had already seated himself on the floor with his back against the far wall and was trying to settle Mickey down onto his lap. She was resisting.

The kitten mewed in irritation. Jimmy tried to pet her into place but she struggled out of his grasp and stalked across the room.

"Am I in the way?" asked Madeline, looking from Jimmy to the kitten. Mickey also looked back and forth between Madeline and Jimmy before turning in a circle and then curling up near the back corner, looking at neither of them.

"Nah," said Jimmy. "You're just fine. If there were another cat in the room, it'd be different, but humans are on a totally different wavelength. I'll tune you out no problem. So, come on. Have a seat. I don't have to actually be physically touching her so long as she's in the same space."

Madeline lowered herself to the floor and tried to fold her legs under her carefully so her short skirt didn't ride up too high. She'd hoped to impress Sam with this dress, just in case she had been back to normal and Madeline had been imagining her strangeness, but now that seemed absurd. Madeline glanced at Jimmy and then at Mickey.

Jimmy straightened his back and closed his eyes, and Madeline knew without being told that she should be perfectly quiet. That part was easy. She was busy trying to memorize everything about this so that she could write it down later and use it in her story. Who'd have thought she'd have met a cat whisperer this evening?

Jimmy pulled in a few deep breaths, and then his breathing went quiet as he lapsed into a meditative state. Madeline felt him go still, then stiller, stiller... She was aware of Mickey's body rising and falling in the corner with each inhalation and exhalation. The kitten snorted once in a larger exhale and deflated like a little furry orange balloon. She was falling asleep. Madeline wasn't sure how many minutes they sat there, and with the wine in her system, she was growing more and more relaxed, until she began to feel sleepy herself. When Jimmy finally spoke Madeline started and bit her tongue—she'd practically forgotten where she was.

"Okay, I'm getting something. It seems she's upset. Seeing you upset her." Above his closed eyes, Jimmy's brow furrowed. "I'm trying to catch why, but it's buried. I don't think she knows. It was like when she saw you pass through the window, she wanted to call to you, but now she wants you to go away. You remind her of her past."

Jimmy opened one eye and peered at Madeline suspiciously before closing it again. "I've had her ever since she was born, and it's not like she's met that many people in her life, but oh well. Maybe she's got you confused with a customer. Hang on, let me see what else I can get. Let's see... Okay... You definitely remind her of someone. I'm getting an image, yeah, that does look like you. Only, in what I'm seeing, you've got long hair."

"I cut it last month," Madeline volunteered, vaguely impressed.

"Well, then that makes sense, I guess. Say, have you come in here before? Maybe while I was gone? I could have had someone else in the shop. This teenage kid that sits in part-time."

"No, never. This is my first time."

Jimmy made a *hmph*-ing sound. "Well, somehow or another, she definitely knows you—and someone else, too. I'm seeing a face, some older looking white guy. He's got a bit of a beard. Tattoos."

Madeline shrugged, trying to ignore the fact that the description sounded like Peter. She was probably reading into it—there were lots of older white guys with beards. "Yeah, I don't know. That could be a lot of people. I mean, there is this one guy, Peter. He's the ex of this woman I know." At the mention of Peter's name, Mickey twitched in her sleep, or at least Madeline thought that she did. "But I don't see how—"

"That could be," Jimmy interrupted. "There's something else that's got her upset. The smell of turkey. Seems like it's giving her a flashback of a Thanksgiving gone wrong, but..." Jimmy scratched his head. "That can't be right. This is her first Thanksgiving. Maybe my mojo is off today. Honestly, I don't know what's wrong. Maybe you are throwing it off, somehow. It's not a full moon out there tonight or something, is it?"

"No."

It was Jimmy's turn to shrug, and he opened his eyes. "Well, then it must be a glitch, but seeing you sure as heck seems to have triggered something in her."

Madeline had a thought that gave her a chill. She tried to shake it off.

"Something happen?" asked Jimmy.

"No, it's nothing."

"You sure? It looked like you got the chills just there."

"No. It's just, well, okay. So this woman I know, Sam—" Mickey's ears twitched in her sleep—"Got into a car accident a few months back..."

"Hang on," interrupted Jimmy again. He held up a finger and squeezed his eyes shut again. "I'm getting something."

Madeline paused, biting her tongue and feeling like she already knew what was coming.

"Okay, this is weird, but I'm seeing a scene of a hospital, and a flash of a woman lying in a bed. She's very still. If I didn't know better, I'd think she might be...well. But Mickey, it feels like she's longing for this person, but at the same time, wants to get away—to be free."

"Fuck," breathed Madeline. This was heavy, and this time she didn't think it was the wine.

"Does that mean something to you?"

"Maybe. How old did you say she was again?"

"Three months."

Madeline crawled across the room until she was in front of the kitten. She observed the delicate face, the jaw, and the softly closed eyes.

"Sam?" Madeline whispered so quietly even she could barely hear it. She placed two fingers on the kitten's head, and it twitched and relaxed beneath her touch. Madeline stroked the kitten's head gently, remembering the feeling of Sam's cheek beneath her hand. A purr rose from the kitten and she lifted her head, leaning into Madeline's touch. When Mickey opened her eyes it was with the eyes of the woman Madeline loved. Sam's had been mottled hazel and the kitten's were yellow, but nevertheless, the being looking out of them was the same.

"Oh, Sam," breathed Madeline. "What in the world happened to you?" She scooped up the kitten and held her close. The kitten curled in Madeline's arms—contented, clueless—and nuzzled her nose into the crook of Madeline's elbow before promptly returning to sleep.

CHAPTER TWENTY-FOUR

IT HAD TAKEN a damn lot of trouble for Peter to arrange those crumbs into place, and when Bianca saw them, what did she do? She stood there, staring, gawking, processing, while precious seconds ticked by. Peter couldn't contain it anymore.

"Hurry up!" he shouted. "She's in trouble! They're in the basement."

Peter had been tracking the Sam-thing's progress ever since he left Rosa's side, a result of a neat trick he'd discovered. Apparently, now that he was dead he possessed the very ghost-like ability to go from one place to another at something like the speed of light. Walls posed no barrier, so he could go just about anywhere, moving through solid objects like, well, a ghost.

"The basement," Bianca muttered, as if the thought had slipped into her mind of its own accord, and she gave a start as if coming back to herself. Had she heard him after all? Peter waved his hands in front of the woman's face, but it was a predictable blank. Maybe it was just a lucky guess.

Bianca shivered and rubbed her hands up and down over her arms as she headed toward the door to the basement stairs.

AUNTIE SAM HAD said they were going to the basement

so no one would notice the missing pie, but Rosa couldn't eat all the pie herself, no matter how she tried. It wasn't even cherry. It was coconut. She didn't understand why Auntie Sam was covered in red.

"Eat and be happy," Auntie Sam kept repeating. "Happy little girl, sweet little girl."

"But I'm full!" Rosa wailed, flinging her fork across the room. A flash of anger like Rosa had never seen before crossed Auntie Sam's face as she moved in a stiff and awkward way to she retrieve the fork.

"No," Auntie Sam said, shoving the fork back into Rosa's hand. Forcing her to clasp it, she wrapped her hand around Rosa's until it curled into a hard, angry fist. "No, you want pie. You *eat* pie."

Rosa started to cry because Auntie Sam hurt her hand, but her tears only made Auntie Sam angrier. She hissed at her to be quiet, pressing a finger over Rosa's lips. Then the finger became two fingers and then these became a hand, covering her nose and mouth and muffling her cries. Rosa struggled against it, kicking and flailing, but Auntie Sam grabbed her harder and her fingernails cut into the side of Rosa's cheeks. Something bad was happening, Rosa realized. Auntie Sam was hurting her. She couldn't breathe. She tried to bite a finger, but Auntie Sam pushed her down roughly. Rosa's head hit the floor. There was an explosion of pain and a brief glimpse of stars, but then Rosa started kicking as hard as she could. She tried to fight Auntie Sam off, but her strength was draining from her.

It felt like she was falling asleep.

Above them, the basement door burst open. Rosa heard feet on the stairs, followed by a familiar voice. "Samantha Belinda Bedford, what the *fuck* is going on down there?" Grandma Bianca yelled from the top of the stairs.

A hazy thought passed through Rosa's mind that her grandma had used a forbidden word and would owe Rosa a dollar later, and then the thought was lost as everything started to darken, the pressure of Auntie Sam's body crushing her against the floor, until all at once the pressure turned into a painful lightness as Auntie Sam rolled off of her. Rosa sucked in air so hard it hurt her ribs and stars of light danced in front of her eyes. Too frightened to weep, she stumbled to her feet, her vision blurring as she tottered over to the stairs where Grandma Bianca rushed down to meet her and wrap her in soft arms. She could feel Auntie Sam's eyes following her the whole way, but she didn't move from where she sat on the floor.

"We were just—" Auntie Sam started to say.

"You were *just?*" Grandma Bianca interrupted her angrily.

"We were just eating pie," Auntie Sam finished. Rosa stole a glance at Auntie Sam and saw that she was smiling her horrible Grinchy smile again. "Weren't we, Rosa?"

"No!" Rosa howled, and using her voice again made her okay enough to start weeping. She wrapped her arms around her grandmother's waist. From upstairs she heard the sound of her mother calling.

"Is that you, Rosa? Honey, where are you?"

"We're down here!" Grandma Bianca yelled back. "In the basement."

Grandma Bianca's arms around Rosa were shaking, and as Rosa continued to peer out at Auntie Sam she decided that the other woman in the basement with them must not be her Auntie Sam at all.

There was more movement upstairs and Rosa heard her dad yelling. He was using the voice he only used when he thought Rosa couldn't hear him, like when he was in the garage swearing at the car or in his bedroom on the phone. "Mom? You've got to come to see this!"

Grandma Bianca didn't move. "Not right now," she yelled back. Her eyes were fixed on the thing that was not Auntie Sam.

Carly arrived, and the little girl transferred her hug to her mother. "Honey, are you okay? What happened?" Carly asked gently, while Rosa blubbered against her shoulder. Then, in her adult voice, "Sam? What the hell is going on?"

"We were eating pie."

"What's this about pie? I can't understand you. Rosa, honey, can you explain?"

Rosa's dad came down the stairs, carrying Diane and followed closely by Grandpa. Now everyone was in the basement. Everyone except Unc—except Peter.

"Mom," Tom said, settling Diane on the floor beside her sister. His voice sounded scared, and she'd never heard her father use that tone before. He drew close to Grandma Bianca and spoke in a whisper in her ear. Rosa couldn't hear what he was saying, but as he talked Grandma Bianca's eyes widened and she clutched his arm like she might fall.

"Carly, girls, it's time to come upstairs," he said, his eyes looking at everyone except Auntie Sam. "We've got to go—now. Move."

"What is it?" Jimmy asked softly, careful not to interrupt what seemed like an important moment between the girl and the cat.

Madeline shook her head, cradling Mickey in her arms. Jimmy waited, giving her a minute before he tried again. "Did I hear you say 'Sam' to her just now? What was that?"

Madeline shook her head again and tucked her chin to her chest. Jimmy could see she was shaking, and then he saw her grow still. She took a deep breath in, let it out, and then she turned to look at him with tears quivering in her eyes.

"I don't know," she said. A tear spilled over and she rebalanced Mickey to flick it away. "I think I got carried away with an idea. Maybe it's true, but I don't know how it could be."

"I believe anything's possible," said Jimmy, and he meant it.

"Tonight I was supposed to go see this woman I know, Sam. She had an accident and fell into a coma three months ago. It took a while, but she woke back up, or at least we thought she did. But after she was awake, she was...different. The Sam I was falling in love with was gone. I think I knew that, but I haven't been able to fully admit it to myself, not until now, because I didn't know where the real Sam had gone, why it wasn't *her* that had woken back up. But now, I do. She's right here." Madeline lifted up the kitten.

"So what you're trying to tell me is that Mickey—"

"Is Sam," Madeline confidently finished for him.

Jimmy considered this. "Well, I'll be. I've never had anything like this happen before, but it makes sense with all those images I was getting of you and that man and that hospital room. If I were a different man, I might be inclined not to believe you, but given that we're both who we are, well, I'm going to have to take you at your word."

"Oh, but it's not my word."

"Now don't go being wishy-washy!" Jimmy couldn't stand it when people couldn't just say what they thought without having to take back their words so many times that they no longer meant anything and might as well have never spoken in the first place.

Madeline said nothing, but her mouth tightened. She returned her gaze to Sam.

"I guess we'd better get used to calling her by her real name," Jimmy said.

"Just like that?" Madeline looked at him in surprise. "Aren't you even sad at all about Mickey? She's not who you thought she was."

"Sad? Now, why would I be sad? I got her name wrong, that's all. If she already had a perfectly good name, then who am I to go around changing it? And if she's still got all those memories, then she must still be Sam."

"But she's a cat!" Madeline cried. As if annoyed, the kitten leapt out of her arms.

"Well, yes," agreed Jimmy. Madeline started to cry in earnest, tears spilling down her cheeks in a rush. "Now, now," he said. "Don't cry, please."

Madeline's tears morphed to anger. "Like, what the fuck!" she shouted, and then instantly lowered her voice as her expression returned to sorrow. "I'm sorry, I'm sorry, I don't want to upset the cats. Oh, I'm sorry! Oh, god, I suck!" Madeline's voice cracked with desperation and Jimmy thought the poor girl was going to lose it.

"Come on, now. If you need it, there's a bathroom out the door and to the left."

"Yeah, okay," Madeline said, seeming to understand what Jimmy meant. She wiped her nose with the back of her hand, heaving and sniffling as tears continued to spill from her eyes. "I guess I should get out of your way. This isn't how I wanted to spend my Thanksgiving." Her tone was accusatory and Jimmy hoped it wasn't directed at him.

She got up and left the room. Immediately the air felt clearer. Jimmy hadn't realized the presence the girl had brought with her.

With a small mew, the kitten that was Sam came to Jimmy, purring against his body with relief.

CHAPTER TWENTY-FIVE

BIANCA WAS TRYING to remain calm because someone in this situation had to and that job was usually assigned to her. Sam had attacked Rosa, and yes, "attacked" was the only word for it. She had also killed Peter. Tom had seen that. Well, not *seen* it, but no one else had gone outside with Peter, and when Tom went out looking he'd found Peter's body lying there, dead and maimed on the street outside under the burnt out streetlamp. Soon, they were going to call the police. Sam would have to be restrained, or kept under watch, and then she would be arrested for murder.

Her daughter would be arrested on Thanksgiving, on the night of her welcome home party, because she had killed her ex-husband and attacked her niece. Bianca was going to remain calm. She was not going to freak out. She would stay in control. Sam would plead mentally unstable, obviously. It was the drugs from the hospital. It had to be. She wasn't herself—she hadn't been since she woke up.

"I'll call the police," Jeff whispered in his wife's ear after Tom and Carly had taken the girls safely back upstairs. His hand closed reassuringly around her arm. "Unless you'd rather do it?"

It took a moment for Bianca to shake her head. "No, I'll stay here with Sam and make sure she's okay."

"Are you sure that's a good idea, staying down here alone with her?"

Bianca gave him a well-practiced look, the one that said *I am your wife and you are not going to tell me what to do.*

Jeff nodded and went upstairs, out of earshot, to make the call. Sam was sitting on the floor, doing nothing, so still and lifeless that it was hard to imagine that just a few moments ago Bianca had seen her trying to smother her own niece. Bianca slowly approached, stopping just out of reach. She was afraid of Sam, she realized. She had been for a while.

"I'm..." Sam started, and Bianca flinched, anticipating the end of the sentence. She had heard enough about how Sam was so damn hungry. She'd gained thirty pounds since she woke up and she ate like an animal.

Bianca forced her voice to sound motherly and not at all scared. "Yes, Sam? What is it?"

"Sor-ry," Sam said slowly, as if she had just discovered the word and was trying it out to see if it worked. Bianca blanched. She couldn't have heard her right. Not now. It was too damn much.

"Excuse me, what did you say?" Bianca heard her tone switch into one that sounded suspiciously like her own mother's. She'd told herself she wouldn't talk like that—but well, look at what had happened, at what Sam had become!

"I'm sorry, Mother," Sam repeated, more firmly the second time, and her voice didn't sound as raspy. It sounded more like Sam.

Bianca turned her back on her daughter. She crossed her arms and made her face tight because she was not going to cry.

"Mother," Sam pleaded behind her.

Bianca crossed her arms tighter. She took deep breaths and counted to ten.

"It was an accident."

"An *accident*!" Bianca whirled around. "It was an *accident* that you killed your ex-husband, that you attacked your favorite niece? It was an *accident*? How does an *accident* like that happen? Can you tell me? Can you?"

"I was…"

Bianca tried to read the expression on Sam's face as she searched for words. What was going on inside that head? Bianca couldn't fathom it.

"I'm afraid that 'accident' isn't going to cut it, sweetie. Not this time. How could you, Sam? How do you expect me to go on now knowing what you've done and what you're going through—in *prison*?"

Bianca felt herself getting choked up as she imagined Sam in some prison cell. She'd be raped, wouldn't she? But maybe she'd like that. God, what was she thinking! She was going insane, becoming as crazy as Sam was.

"I don't even know who you are anymore," Bianca found herself speaking more words she'd sworn off.

"I'm Sam," Sam said simply. "Still Sam. Sam I Am."

Rage and laughter and grief fought for dominance in Bianca but only a frustrated sigh issued from her lips. How could Sam joke at a time like this?

"It was the drugs, wasn't it?" said Bianca, grasping. "It's that stuff the hospital insisted we give you. It made you..."

"Hungry."

Bianca flinched. "Yes, all right, fine. It made you hungry, but you didn't know what you were doing when you were out there with Peter just now, did you?"

"No," Sam agreed.

"I knew it," Bianca sighed. "Maybe you'll get off easy... Twenty years or..."

Bianca's jaw trembled as she did a quick mental calculation. She might be dead in twenty years; she'd be over seventy. A barking laugh, a mad sound, escaped from within and a couple of tears spilled down her cheeks. She brushed them away. So, this was where it all ended.

"You know what, sweetie? I'd probably have killed him, too, if I were you," Bianca admitted as she looked at her daughter, sitting so meekly on the floor. "God. I just never thought it would come to this. Not you, not my Sam. How did you even do it?"

Sam started to lift her hands and Bianca's eyes were drawn to Sam's stiff fingers. They tightened around something invisible, squeezed it, but Bianca barely had time to register this before Sam lowered her hands down again.

"I don't know," Sam said simply. Her voice was hoarse, but where before Bianca had thought the hoarseness was some change caused by the coma, now she thought it was the result of pain. Sam felt bad about what she'd done, didn't she?

"No, of course you don't," Bianca agreed. "You were delusional. Psychotic. We're going to get you off those meds, starting now." She didn't say anything about the fact that it was clearly too late, that she'd be taken to prison and by then the question of meds would be irrelevant.

"Mother," Sam said, "I don't want to go away."

"Well, I don't want you to go away either, darling, but at this point, I'm afraid we're not left with much of a choice."

Sam said nothing, and Bianca looked at her, thinking. It was obvious Sam hadn't been herself. It was obvious Sam would never intentionally harm someone. It was obvious that taking her to a prison cell would be an injustice, that no one would understand her there—no one would listen, no one would know. There was the back exit from the basement, and if she and her daughter slipped out together quickly...

"Mother," Sam said again, using this infuriating form of address that was so child-like and formal. "I know they're going to take me away, but first, do you think we can go for a drive together—please?"

Perhaps it was that the request was so perfectly formulated, so very like Bianca had always imagined Sam would be in a crisis, that she found herself wondering, what was *really* the harm? Sam ought to be allowed to get out of the house, to enjoy a final half hour of being with her mom, before...

Bianca's purse was upstairs, along with her keys. She'd have to go grab it.

"All right," she said, calculating in her head how she'd nip up to the entryway, grab her purse, and return unnoticed. "I'll be back in a minute. Don't you dare move a muscle. Stay put."

CHAPTER TWENTY-SIX

PETER HAD SAVED the girl, or he felt like he had. Maybe it had been chance that Bianca had gone into the basement, but Peter fancied it was because of him. Now that the Sam-thing had been stopped, he was unsure of what to do. Hang around, he supposed. See what happened next.

And then it was just him, Bianca, and Sam—the awkward trio. He knew they gossiped about him, had been doing so for years—but that comment about killing him? That one had hurt.

Peter half-expected the creature to jump up and go running the second Bianca left the room, but it didn't. It just sat there, unmoving. How the fuck had it gotten here and taken over Sam? What was it planning to do now? Did it even have a plan?

A moment later Bianca returned and the two women snuck out the back door to where Bianca's car was waiting. Peter didn't have to sneak. This was his dream, after all… or rather, his death. He finally got to control things, to go with the flow. That was what Sam had always encouraged him to do—*"Stop being so stiff, Peter. Just relax, Peter. Come on, Peter."*—as if she'd been any better.

The night was dark and the women seemed cold. At least Bianca did, she was shivering. It was hard to tell with the other. From inside the house came the sounds of bustling and movement, and Peter watched the lighted windows, remembering the night's earlier events as if *those* had been the dream, rather than this, now. Had that been him, earlier, sitting down to a cheerful Thanksgiving dinner, or had that been someone else? Who was he now, anyway?

Nobody. He was a dead man, and frankly he wasn't sure if he cared.

Peter sat in the back seat while the women rode in front. When the engine turned on the radio automatically filled the cab with the sound of a talk show, but Bianca quickly turned it off. No one seemed to breathe—not that Peter needed to—until they were out on the road, and then it was as if they all heaved a collective sigh. They hadn't been caught. They had gotten away. Peter wasn't sure if that was a good thing, but at least it was less complicated.

With the radio off, it only took a few seconds for the silence to become oppressive. If anyone could have heard Peter, he'd have tried to crack a joke.

Well, this is a dark night. Why all the dead faces? Look more lively!

Ha.

Bianca was first to speak. "Remember, Sam, that you don't have to talk to anyone if you don't want to. We'll get you a lawyer, someone who knows what we should do."

Sam said nothing in response, which probably infuriated Bianca, but Peter knew why. It was because the thing in the front seat was not really Sam and probably didn't give a damn about the fate of the body it had stolen. If only he could warn Bianca.

"You know, Bianca," Peter said out loud. "That isn't really Sam sitting next to you. It's something else, I'm sorry to say. What kind of something, you ask? To be honest, I haven't figured it out, but some kind of monster is my best guess."

No reaction, just as Peter had expected. But then Sam turned slowly and looked to the back seat, her eyes staring right into where his were supposed to be. It had heard him. Despite the fact that was dreaming, or dead, or whatever, that monster had heard what he'd said.

"What is it, honey? Did something happen?" Bianca asked, glancing sideways at Sam as she flicked the signal switch, turning onto Main Street.

The monster smiled and turned to face front again, just as slowly as it had craned its head back, and said in its new slow, careful English, "Nothing, Mother."

Nothing, Mother, Peter mocked.

Oh, fuck you, monster.

"WHAT IS IT, honey? Did something happen?" Bianca asked.

"Nothing, Mother," the ghost said. It had killed Peter,

and that should have gotten rid of him, but now the man's consciousness was tagging along, refusing to do as most dead things did and stay with his body or move along to somewhere else. Maybe it was because the ghost had taken his eyes. Maybe that had been a mistake, and the action had tied Peter to the ghost somehow. Whatever the reason, Peter had gotten stuck in the ghost's web like some kind of fly. The ghost would try to avoid such an unpleasant scenario next time. It had tried to enjoy a real meal with the little girl but it had been stopped so abruptly.

It *had* to feed again. It would go slower this time. It would get it right.

"Mother," said the ghost, and it waited for Bianca's response. Bianca kept her eyes on the road, not giving the ghost her attention. The ghost waited patiently, staring at her intently.

"What?" asked Bianca at last.

"I'm sorry, Mother."

"You said that before!" exclaimed Bianca, exasperated. "What do you want me to do, forgive you?"

The ghost continued to stare, watching Bianca's lips tremble and her eyes water. Her jaw moved as she fought to maintain control.

"All right," she swallowed, "I'll grant that you're sorry. I'll grant that. I'll grant that what you did was a horrible, stupid mistake, and it will never, ever happen again—it had better not, not if you ever want me to be able to look at you again."

"Of course, Mother."

"Good." Bianca heaved a shaking sigh, finally allowing herself a glance at Sam. A tear spilled from one eye and she hurriedly wiped it away. "Not that it matters now, anyway. What's done is done and you're going to prison. This is going to be our goodbye. So, first, take this,"— she reached for something in her purse and handed her phone to the ghost—"and put it somewhere I can't hear it. I can't bear to listen to it vibrating when they realize we're gone. Now, tell me, Sam, just pretend things are normal for a second. Is there somewhere you want to see before they lock you up? Somewhere you want to go before you're stuck in a tiny little cell where you can hardly move?"

The ghost carefully put the phone into its pocket. It had been waiting for this question, and it knew just where they should go. "To the lake."

"To the where?"

"To my house. To the lake."

"To your... Sam, I'm surprised at you. I didn't know you even remembered."

The ghost smiled to itself. It had heard many things during its convalescence. The Sam who had used to live in this body had been quite fond of the place called the lake house. It would be quiet and private there, the ghost was certain. It would be the perfect place to enjoy Bianca.

PETER'S BRAIN RUSHED forward quickly. She wanted to go

to the lake house. It would be secluded and no one would come around looking for them. It would be the perfect place to...

No. The bitch wouldn't.

But she would because this wasn't Sam. This was whatever *thing* that now inhabited Sam's body. It had already killed him. It had tried to smother Rosa. He would be stupid to think it wouldn't hurt Bianca, too.

Peter took a deep breath, preparing to call out to Bianca, but that had been futile before. It would only alert the monster to his plans. *Okay, Peter. Think, think, think.*

He elevated himself out of the car, started to rise up, and then realized he didn't know where he was going. He sank back down quickly. He didn't want to lose them.

Damn it, Peter. Back to the drawing board. How could he stop Sam?

Sam.

His mind kept going back to Sam. This was another thing that was bothering him. If there was a monster in Sam's body then where the hell was Sam? If Peter was here, then certainly Sam must be *somewhere*, right? She couldn't have vanished? She couldn't be gone?

The thought struck Peter as incomprehensibly horrible. If Sam were gone from the world, it would mean this really was hell, because in as long as Peter had lived he'd never met someone so good. That was the truth, the real truth—the truth that lurked behind his thoughts of how much of a bitch she'd been. Sam had loved him more than anyone when nobody else could even see him. Sam had saved the small light of his soul from the darkness he was trying to drown it in. He was consoled by his knowledge that somewhere out there was that goodness, was Sam as he'd known her.

Sam had never loved him the way he'd loved her. He wasn't a fool, he could see that. She'd loved him in her way, sure, but she'd never doted on his existence like her life depended on him. She didn't know what that felt like. She couldn't understand.

Peter deserved it. All of it—the heartbreak, the imbalance—and Sam had deserved his admiration, while he'd done nothing to deserve hers. For years he'd wanted nothing more than to become worthy of her praise, but the more he'd grasped after it the farther away it had gone. The more impossible the task had grown.

Now, Peter knew, he would never succeed at getting Sam to love him. After all, he was dead, wasn't he? It was time he just admitted it. And so, very likely, was she.

And God, what a memory of him she'd have if she was still *somewhere*. She'd see pictures in the news: his eyeless body dead in street.

Disgusting, she'd think*, so that's how Peter ended up. I knew he would.*

No, that was too hard on her. He knew Sam would feel more than that. Of course, she'd try not to, she'd try to bury it like she always did.

It was the main talent she'd honed over the years their

marriage had been failing. She'd become a master at suppressing what she was feeling. The more he'd tried to get her to not do that, the deeper she'd buried her heart—the farther away she'd gone. So Peter understood. In a way, it was all his fault. He'd pushed her away long before she'd ever had the chance to leave.

But I do remember, Peter, he could almost hear Sam saying. *I didn't forget we were happy once. That's what makes me so sad.*

It was like he could hear her, like he could actually feel where she was in the universe. Yes, that was her he felt, out there. He was certain of it. And she was not too far, not too far at all.

Peter closed his eyes, and behind them was a map of the universe. There were two glowing dots—one was him and the other Sam. He watched as one of the dots—his—moved down the streets of Boston while the other remained still. She was six-point-four miles away. Somehow he knew that, like Google Maps for the brain. Another neat trick he seemed to have picked up, like moving through walls.

Keeping his eyes closed, Peter lifted out of the car. He'd find her, the real Sam. He'd try to let her know what had happened, and maybe together they could stop the beast in time.

CHAPTER TWENTY-SEVEN

MADELINE LOCKED HERSELF in a tiny little bathroom that smelled of litter and cat urine and turned on the light. She stole a glance at herself in the mirror and burst into fresh tears.

Sam would rather become a cat than give Madeline a chance. Oh, fuck her, the fucking bitch. A cat!

Indulging in a moment of self-pity, Madeline sat on the toilet and sniffled into a handful of tissue, then she got up, washed her hands, and dabbed away the mascara pooling under her eyes. In her reflection, Madeline's jaw trembled as she imagined everything she'd wanted to tell Sam in person. She'd wanted to say, *Hey*. She'd wanted to say, *I'm sorry*. She'd wanted to say, *I love you, no matter what*. But now she couldn't say that, not in a way that Sam would hear, because Sam was a fucking cat.

Madeline dabbed her eyes. She needed to clean herself up. She needed to get back out there. She needed to apologize to Jimmy, get out of there and go home where things made more sense. There was an ending to her story working itself out in her mind, and she needed to finish things. It was time.

Checking herself once more in the mirror, a gasp lodged itself in Madeline's throat. There was someone in the room behind her. She couldn't see him, not clearly, and it was gone in a blink, but she'd seen it.

Peter.

There was nothing there, nothing aside from a towel hung on a rack, but that wasn't a person. It must have been a trick of the light, or her imagination running away with her. Madeline rubbed at her eyes. She was feeling a little emotional, but it wasn't a problem, she was fine. She checked her reflection in the mirror one last time, leaning in close to wipe her eyes, but as she did her breath fogged up the glass, revealing a swirl of letters that evaporated nearly as quickly as they appeared.

S. A. M. Sam.

Madeline screamed.

JIMMY HEARD THE girl shrieking and braced himself. The noise had scared little Sam and all her claws were out, carving tiny red scratches on the skin of his forearm.

A moment later Madeline rushed back into the room. She'd been crying, from the look of it, and her face was a vision of terror.

"In the bathroom…"

Jimmy rushed to his feet at once. "Do I need to go check it out?"

"No…yes! Maybe. There was…"

Jimmy placed Sam on the floor and she followed on his heels as he strode down the hall to the bathroom,

Madeline hot behind them. He pushed the door open so hard it banged against the wall. The light was still on. "Hello?" he demanded.

"It's not... It was here," said Madeline, still gasping. She pointed at the mirror, and Jimmy noticed her hand was shaking. "I was washing my hands, and I leaned in a little close and I got some breath on the mirror, like fog you know, and right in front of my eyes someone wrote *Sam*."

Jimmy peered in close to the mirror, looking for a trace of evidence, some kind of fingerprint smudges, but there was nothing to prove or falsify her story.

Jimmy pondered. It didn't get him very far. "Okay," he said.

"Yeah." Madeline was wringing her hands now.

"So," said Jimmy, "you think it was a... Well, just what do you think it was?"

Madeline became excitable. "Okay, so, for just a second, I thought it was a trick of my eyes, but I think I saw Peter."

"Peter. And that's...?"

"Sam's ex-husband. The kinda beardy guy with tattoos."

"The one I was picking up on earlier."

"Right."

"You think this was him, then? Writing her name on the mirror?"

"I don't know!" Madeline cried, her voice edging on hysteria.

Jimmy patted the air with his palms in a motion of calm. "Okay, okay. It's all right. It doesn't look like there's anything more to see in here, so why don't we all go back to where we were and think."

Jimmy flipped off the light and ushered Madeline and Sam back into the little carpeted room. Sam didn't seem too keen on going back in there and tried to wander away, but Jimmy nudged her through the door with the toe of his shoe. Once inside, he sat down and indicated that Madeline should do the same. They sat facing each other on the floor, with Sam idling around back and forth between them.

"A ghost?" suggested Jimmy after the space of a few quiet minutes.

Madeline groaned.

"Well, we have to throw some ideas out there. Weren't you talking about a ghost when you first came in?"

"No!" she scoffed, and then reconsidered. "I mean, yes, but that was a different kind of ghost, I think, and a story, not a real thing. This might be a... I don't know. Some kind of manifestation, or a trick. Maybe Peter is doing a spell somewhere, trying to send us a message or something, right?"

Jimmy raised an eyebrow and spoke slowly. "Peter is doing a spell?"

Madeline groaned again and shrugged. She knew it sounded insane.

"Okay, sure," Jimmy offered. "Could be something like that."

"Or…"

"Or what?"

"Nothing. Just… In this story I'm writing…" Madeline shook her head. "But stories aren't real." She looked at Jimmy like she was looking for confirmation so Jimmy nodded, though he didn't really know what she was getting at.

She didn't continue.

"If this story is somehow connected to Sam, maybe you'd better talk through what you're thinking," he suggested.

Madeline nodded hesitantly. "Right, so, I'm writing a story about a ghost. A hungry ghost."

"A hungry ghost! Well, I suppose Thanksgiving's a good time for it to find something to eat."

"Exactly, that's what I thought. So, this ghost has been slowly taking over Sam's life. It's stolen her body and it's been eating non-stop, but now it's discovering that it's not satisfied with food. It wants to eat people, too. And so Peter, Sam's ex-husband, is always around, and he seems like an easy target. It's like he's practically begging to be taken."

"So the ghost gobbles him up."

Madeline nodded slowly. "Possibly."

"But if the ghost has gobbled him up, then how would he be here now?"

"What if he didn't die completely? If his consciousness somehow lingered…"

"What you're saying," clarified Jimmy, "is that he too became a ghost, which brings us right back to the idea of ghosts again."

"Let's say it is a ghost, but a different kind of ghost—one that wants to talk to us. What would Peter want? Why would he be here?"

"Something to do with Sam?" suggested Jimmy. Madeline nodded.

"Yeah. Like, I was thinking about how he was probably at that party tonight, the one at Sam's house. So, what if something happened at the party?"

"That could be," said Jimmy, "and now he needs to send us a message."

"Exactly. A message—something to do with Sam. But how could we figure it out what it is?"

Jimmy thought on it. "I know! There are those boards, what are they called, Ouija boards? Old wooden things, supposed to be able to communicate with ghosts."

"Sure, but we'd need to have a board."

A smile spread across Jimmy's face.

"What?" asked Madeline, but Jimmy just kept on smiling. "What?"

MADELINE WAITED WHILE Jimmy fetched the board. This was the single weirdest night of her entire life. Once in a while, in her life, certain things had lined up in ways that seemed like fate. There'd been little coincidences here and there that seemed like signs, but for the most part, life moved on and it was totally impossible to follow. All sorts of things happened for God knows why and it was all she could do to survive. Tonight was different. Things were headed in one direction. It was like Madeline was riding in a boat and Jimmy was in it, and other people were, too. Sam and Peter and maybe others, who knew, and together they were all trying to keep the thing afloat. It was unbelievable, but here she was.

Jimmy returned with the board and set it down on the carpet. Sam pounced on it, batting at the planchette.

"No, no," said Jimmy, pushing her off of the board's wooden surface. She protested a little, trying to get at it again, but Jimmy resolutely held her off and eventually she gave up. Madeline watched this with confusion. Where was Sam in that little cat?

"What do you think she's thinking, trying to get on there? Do you think she wants to contact Peter?"

"I think she wants to play with our fun new toy," Jimmy said, and then he looked at Madeline, who looked horrified. "I'm sorry," he shrugged, although he didn't really look sorry, "but even if she is Sam, the truth is she's also a cat."

Madeline didn't breathe for a second, and then ever so slowly she exhaled. She was going to let that go. She wasn't going to think about it.

"Okay," said Madeline, "Fine. How do we work this thing?"

CHAPTER TWENTY-EIGHT

PETER HAD ARRIVED at what should have been Sam's location, but all he'd discovered was that skinny home-wrecker Madeline and some black guy hanging out with a cat. Were his calculations off? He'd tried to question Madeline to see if she knew where Sam was, but she'd just freaked out. Still, perhaps if he hung around long enough, he'd figure out why he was here.

Peter watched the unlikely pair get out a Ouija board and set it up. He had no idea if things like that actually worked. So far he'd had some semi-successful attempts at communication— rearranging the crumbs, leaving the marks on the glass—but he had no idea if he could move that little pointer around on the board. He sat down on one side, between Madeline and Jimmy.

"What you do," Jimmy was explaining to Madeline, "is we both rest two fingers very lightly on one side of the planchette, and then we wait for something to move it."

"Why do we have to be touching it?" Madeline asked. "I mean, if there's a ghost in here couldn't he just move it himself?"

"I don't know," said Jimmy, "all I know is that's what the instructions said. And if there's one thing I've learned in life, it's that if you want good results, you'd better follow the instructions. No improvising until you've got the hang of the basics."

"Okay," said Madeline, and they both rested their fingers on the planchette as Jimmy had instructed. Just for fun, Peter reached out and did the same. If he engaged his muscles, he could feel them hover right at the line of resistance that defined the barrier of the object. If he exerted just a little more pressure, however, he'd pass right through.

"And now?" asked Madeline.

"Now," said Jimmy, "we ask a question. Where do you think we should start?"

"How about with 'Are you Peter?' since it's a basic yes or no question?"

At the outer edges of the board, the words *Yes* and *No* were written, and Peter saw that he should have been able to move the marker to either of them in response. However, when he tried to push the pointer, his fingers passed right through it. He tried again, and again, each time with no success. He cursed to himself. Was he doing this wrong? He just wanted the damn thing to say *yes*!

As he watched, the planchette started to move.

"Hey, it's moving," said Jimmy.

"Yeah, it is," agreed Madeline, her voice incredulous.

Peter watched as the pointer slid across the board. It varied in between heading toward *Yes* or *No* as if uncertain, and then, shakily, it sped across the board to *Yes*.

"Yes," said Madeline.

"Yes," confirmed Jimmy.

They looked at each other and Peter felt sort of useless.

"Okay, what next?" said Madeline. "What else should we ask?"

"I don't know," said Jimmy. "How about, let's see, 'Do you have a message for us'?"

They reset the planchette in the middle of the board. Madeline closed her eyes this time and so did Jimmy. "Do you have a message for us, Peter?" Madeline whispered, unnecessarily, since Peter had heard the question the first time. He found himself watching Madeline and thinking how unfair it was that she'd tried to steal Sam from him when she had such an advantage. It wasn't like he could compete with her—she was so young, so beautiful—and he'd always suspected Sam had been more attracted to women than men anyway. He hadn't stood a chance, and things had already been shaky.

In a way, this was all her fault. He'd fucked up with Sam, but Madeline had sealed the deal.

The pointer zoomed to *Yes*.

Madeline opened her eyes, and Peter couldn't help but wonder if they'd ever seen Sam naked. "Yes," Madeline read, and for a second she almost saw him, looking at her, but her gaze passed through his. "What's the message?" asked Madeline, resetting the planchette.

Peter realized it *was* him pushing the planchette, not with his fingers but with his thoughts.

"*B*," read Madeline, calling out the letters as the pointer moved, Peter's mind brushing the planchette across the board as surely as Madeline's fingers had brushed across Sam's skin. *I* it moved again. "A... N... C... A... Bianca. Bianca. That's Sam's mom," Madeline was explaining to the man. "Bianca... *I... S...* Bianca is... *I... N... T... R... O...* Bianca is in trouble? Yes. Bianca is in trouble. What kind of trouble? How? Where? *A... T...* at... *T... H...* At the... *L... A... K... E... H... O... U...* At the lake house—that's Sam's place—but why there? Don't answer that. Well, what can we do? What do we do?"

"You know this lake house?" interjected Jimmy.

"Well, yeah," said Madeline, blushing as she remembered her plans for Sam in that place. "I mean, I have the address."

"Well, let's go."

"Okay, but wait, maybe first..."

"What is it?" said Jimmy.

"Well, shouldn't we ask him if there's anything else we need to know?"

"Sure."

Madeline asked, looking up into the room pleadingly as she closed her eyes. Peter wondered if Madeline had loved Sam, too, as much as he had loved her. No, he knew she had, just in a different way. He wasn't sure if he could tell her what had happened to Sam, or to him. He wasn't even sure if he could admit it to himself.

The planchette sped to *Yes* without Peter even realizing he had thought it, and then he watched with horror as it went on to spell out the rest.

Madeline read the result out loud: "*I'm dead*. Peter's dead." She looked up at Jimmy. "Well, I guess now we know."

"Fuck," said Peter. The truth had been stolen from his subconscious whether he liked it or not and Madeline had narrated it out for him. He guessed he'd just have to accept it.

CHAPTER TWENTY-NINE

BIANCA WAS BEGINNING to feel like this wasn't such a good idea. She'd acted hastily, impulsively, wanting to stop time. Bianca was sure that back at the house her family would be going crazy trying to reach her. They'd probably have assumed the worst—that Sam had done to her what she'd already done to Peter.

Bianca shuddered. That was impossible. There was no way Sam could overpower her, even if she wanted to. She was all bark and no bite. And yet, she'd managed somehow with Peter. Of course, Sam had been holding on to such anger with that man, not that it was any justification. Bianca was Sam's mother. Sam wouldn't hurt her mother. That had to still be true.

But then Bianca remembered what had happened in the basement with Rosa.

"Look," said Bianca, clearing her throat and hoping Sam didn't hear the fear in her voice. "It's going to have to be a quick stop at the house. You can say goodbye to your old things, maybe grab a book that I'll try to get to you. Anyway, you can still write, can't you, after you're all locked up? Your life isn't over. You can still accomplish a lot. Maybe you'll write a book."

Next to her, Sam stared silently through the windshield,

which made Bianca extremely uncomfortable. They took the highway out of Boston, headed for Lakeville, and Bianca tried to ignore the feeling in the pit of her stomach that was telling her to turn back around. She'd promised Sam a drive. She'd offered to take her where she wanted. She'd follow it through.

"Do you remember," asked Bianca, "the first time we took you to the ocean? You were six years old, and you jumped into the water and started flailing around, splashing like mad. I was afraid you were drowning, but after I wrestled you out of the water you looked up at me with those big hazel eyes, lashes all wet, and said in that faint British accent you were putting on then, 'Mummy, why did you stop me? I was turning into a fish!' You were always so creative. You'd pretend to be a fish and then a dolphin. Then it was a mermaid rescuing sinking ships. You always had a good heart, Sam, right from the very beginning."

Bianca wrapped the memory around her, trying to find comfort in it. Little Sam, golden-haired and tanned, covered in salt water and sand. She'd had the most fantastic curls back then, but she'd grown out of them, as she had so many other things. Bianca's heart ached as she looked at Sam in the seat next to her. After a pause Sam stared back at her, oncoming lights from a passing car briefly illuminating her face. For a split second, Bianca thought she saw something that was not her daughter sitting beside her. Her breath caught in her throat, and

Bianca turned her eyes back to the road, trying to be rational as she considered how much farther they had to travel before arriving at the lake house. Forty minutes, she guessed, and she suddenly wasn't sure she could make it. She shouldn't have agreed to go so far out of the way. She should have called Jeff and let the rest of her family know where she was.

They'd have told her to come back right away. They'd have said that she'd gone mad—and they might have been right. She should go back...

Her heart pounded in her chest and she tried to force it to subside. *Calm down!* Bianca scolded herself. *You're forty minutes away. You'll swing by the lake house quickly and then you'll turn back around and take Sam straight to the police station.*

IN THE SEAT beside Bianca, the ghost could tell the woman was growing suspicious. For a second—just a second—Bianca had seen its true face. The ghost would have to be careful; it would have to play nice. If it wanted to keep its human existence it would have to formulate a plan. This was difficult for the ghost, planning. It had never had the luxury. It had always been driven by hunger and the need to satisfy itself. That immediacy had eliminated the ability to think long-term. It couldn't even remember how it had ended up a hungry ghost in the first place. It seemed it had always been that way, but that couldn't have been true.

"Bianca," said the ghost, and then it realized its error. "Mother."

"Yes?" said Bianca, glancing sidelong at the ghost.

"What do you think happened to Peter? I mean, what happens after we die?"

"Oh, my," said Bianca, and her forehead wrinkled. "Well, I suppose he's gone to Heaven."

"Heaven? What's that?"

"You know very well that I don't know."

The ghost was silent, waiting her out. Eventually, she sighed, shook her head, and spoke again. "Come on, Sam. Heaven is a story from the Bible, something we tell ourselves to make death sound better, but if you want to know what I think, well, I guess we probably go back to some cosmic beginning. Some time before we were individual people, back when we were all just soul, no separate you or separate me. Maybe that's a kind of heaven in itself." She took a breath. "I believe Peter's at peace now, or at least no longer suffering."

"I don't think so," countered the ghost. "I don't think he was ready for peace. I think he had unfinished business, and that once he finishes that, he'll become something else."

This seemed to frustrate the mother. "Well if you already think all that, then what the hell are you asking me for?" she snapped.

"Because I wanted to know why people become what they do—why things are what they are."

"You're being cryptic, Sam. Be specific or else I can't help you."

"Why did you get born as you? Why did I get born as...this?"

"Because you're my daughter, and I love you, and you were always meant to be my daughter. Isn't that enough, Sam? Why do you need more reason than that? What if there is no other reason? What if things just are, and there is no 'why'?"

The ghost was silent. Bianca didn't understand. She hadn't seen Peter's ghost. She didn't know of the realm of the hungry ghosts. The ghost had a new sense of fear that was rising up. It tried to ignore this feeling, but there was a warning growing that could not be ignored. Still, the ghost couldn't turn back now.

They were nearly at the lake. The ghost was not Sam, and it was tired of pretending that it was.

CHAPTER THIRTY

MADELINE NAVIGATED AS they drove out of Boston in Jimmy's car, reciting the directions from her phone's screen and telling Jimmy when to switch lanes. Boston streets could change quickly and if you missed your turn you could easily get pulled off course. There wasn't time to get lost.

"Up there," she said, pointing. "After this block, it's your turn."

They took the highway out of the city and sped southeast toward Lakeville. Sam sat, amiably enough, on Madeline's lap as they drove, mostly dozing. It hadn't felt right to try to put her in a carrier. Madeline wasn't sure they should be bringing Sam the kitten with them since it wasn't like she could fully understand what was going on, but it seemed cruel to leave her behind if her mom was in danger, even if technically Sam had a new feline mother that had given her a new life. As a cat.

Madeline didn't know what they were going to do when they arrived at the lake house. She'd been planning some grand rescue mission, some exorcism or something that would get the hungry ghost out of Sam, but how was she supposed to put Sam back where she belonged if she was a cat? Nothing was right. This wasn't the story she had meant to write, but it was too late to change it now. Apparently, it was happy to write itself.

Jimmy put on some music, even though it wasn't really appropriate. Still, Madeline figured there was no use in upsetting Sam, and if Madeline remained calm, then Sam would, too. Either they'd get there in time or they wouldn't. There was no point in getting worked up about it. All she could do was deal with what came next.

THE LAKE THAT lined the street that led to Sam's house appeared to be frozen. The snow had finally stopped and the sky overhead had started to clear, the moonlight reflecting off the lake's icy surface. What a Thanksgiving— the lake had frozen, and along with it, hell had frozen over, too. Yet in the crisp cleanness of it all, it was hard not to feel a sense of hope, and as Bianca pulled into Sam's driveway and parked the cold air that rushed into her lungs gave her a queer feeling.

Maybe this is all a dream, she thought, and it almost seemed possible.

She turned and looked at Sam.

"Do you have your key?" she asked.

Sam stared at her, not comprehending her question, or perhaps pretending to not understand.

"Don't worry," said Bianca, shaking her head. "I have my spare." She hadn't thought Sam would remember, but it would have been nice to be surprised.

The stairway to the porch was covered in slippery snow. Bianca brushed powder from the handrail and gripped it firmly as she went up. At the doorway, she shifted through her keys. There was a key to Tom's house, a key for her own house, a key for the shed, and there, Sam's key—short, simple, and nubby. It felt precious in Bianca's hand as she fitted it into the lock. The lock was frozen, but she forced it, gripping with both hands. She could feel Sam behind her, waiting, hovering, standing so close she could feel her breath cool against her neck. Shouldn't Sam's breath have been warm? Well, maybe it was the wind. Regardless, it was time to get this over with.

Bianca opened the door and held it back for Sam to enter.

"You first," said Sam.

"Oh, dear, don't be silly. Come on, now. It's cold."

Sam waited—stubborn thing!—but eventually went inside. What had gotten into her? Killing Peter, asking about Heaven... Was it some kind of existential crisis? It was just ridiculous, the idea of Sam killing someone. By the time they got back someone would have realized it had all been a mistake. Peter had fallen or else he had done it himself. He had threatened to kill himself more than once, after all. It wouldn't really be a surprise. Sam, wanting to protect Peter, was probably trying to take the blame for it out of some noble impulse.

Bianca was becoming very good at lying to herself.

She flicked on the lights. "Okay, love. Here we are.

Go on in, have a look, see if there's a book you want and some clothes, maybe." Bianca wasn't sure they let you bring your own clothes to jail, which seemed strangely inhumane.

Bianca tried to picture Sam in an orange jumper, and it was unfortunately easy for her to do. She'd look like one of those women on *Orange is the New Black*. She'd probably make friends, get into trouble. It wouldn't even be all that bad. It may even be a little fun being around all those interesting women. Sam was a survivor. She'd find a place for herself anywhere, trade poems for cigarettes, and make art out of suffering. They'd love her. She'd be popular. She always was. But Sam wouldn't be anywhere near Bianca, and that was what broke Bianca's heart most.

Bianca was spacing out, staring at a vase on the table in front of the side window. The vase was blue and elegantly curved, filled with flowers that had long ago wilted. No one had been in the house for four months, not since the night Sam had gotten in the accident—the night that had changed everything.

"Mother."

Bianca turned at the sound of Sam's voice behind her.

"Mother, I…"

Sam stared at her. When had her daughter ever been at a loss for words? For most of her life, she hadn't been able to either stop talking or slow down. Whether it was this place or the trick of the light in the car, the truth of it all finally hit Bianca. Sam had never woken up from that accident. The figure in front of her was a stranger. She may have had Sam's eyes, her nose, and her pouting mouth, the tiny little gap between her front teeth that gave her face its unique character, but with her emaciated body and protruding stomach and the strange, soulless expression she always wore, it was impossible to reconcile the creature in front of her with the daughter she had loved.

"Sam, what is it?" said Bianca at last, speaking to the Sam that had once made this place a home and not the thing in front of her. "What is it that you want from me?"

"Mother," said Sam, and she stepped forward, reaching out. Instinctively, Bianca stepped backward, but then forced herself to stand still. She would not move away as she allowed Sam to come closer and place her hand on her chest. Bianca could feel Sam's cold fingers pulling the warmth from her body as a chill seeped through her sweater.

Bianca swallowed. She placed one hand on top of her daughter's icy one.

Sam kept staring at her with those dark and needful eyes, and Bianca felt her own filling with uncomprehending tears.

"Oh, Sam, what the hell happened to you?"

"Something terrible," said Sam, her voice raspy and not her own, and Bianca's heart broke.

"What do you want? What can I give you?"

"You."

Bianca felt her entire being come undone with a single pull.

CHAPTER THIRTY-ONE

PETER WAS TRACKING their progress as they closed in on Bianca. The one thing he couldn't figure was what had happened to Sam. Where was she now? And why couldn't he find her when he'd been certain she'd be somewhere in that pet store?

He'd heard Madeline and Jimmy say Sam's name a few times, and for some damn reason they'd brought along a cat. One of them had even called the cat "Sam," which was a stupid sort of coincidence. Had he found a cat named Sam instead of his ex-wife? What kind of lame ass trick was it if his dead-man superpower didn't even work correctly?

He slid through the roof of the car and transported himself to the lake house only to find that Bianca and Sam had already arrived. Even worse, they were already inside. Looking through a window along the wall by the lake he saw the monster closing in on Bianca. Gasping, he flitted as quickly as light back to Madeline and Jimmy, who had just taken the exit for Lakeville and were mere minutes away from the house.

"Shit!" he cried, re-entering the backseat. "We've got to hurry! They're already there. Can't this thing go any faster? We've got a clear road ahead!" He pounded one fist against the seat in front of him and was infuriated by the lack of impact as his hand slid through. "Damn it!"

As usual, no one heard him, but Madeline shifted uncomfortably in her seat, almost as if she'd felt something. She scratched her nose. She cocked her head, and then she took a careful breath in and cleared her throat noisily.

Jimmy glanced at her. "Did something happen?"

"I was just wondering, could you go a bit faster? I don't mean to rush, it's just...I feel like we need to hurry."

Bianca knew, even though she couldn't explain it, that even though Sam was standing directly in front of her, her daughter was dead.

She knew it with such certainty that it seemed to her as if she must have known it for a long time already and been in denial. Bianca had been delusional, convincing herself Sam was still herself when it was clear—painfully clear—that whoever was looking out from behind her daughter's eyes was not in any way the child she'd given birth to.

"You," the false Sam hissed at her. "You. I want you."

I want my mom! Bianca remembered Sam screaming as a toddler, so many years ago, her tiny fingers balled into fists, eyes screwed up tight.

"Oh," said Bianca, and it was the only word she could utter. If she opened her lips, a cry would escape. It required all of her willpower to stop herself from keeling over. There was a storm in her chest, but she would remain standing.

"Mother," said Sam, and her hand slid up to Bianca's face to rest on her cheek. "I am so hungry. I need you...."

Bianca was going to throw up. She was being turned inside out. She remembered Sam being born. She was being inverted in reverse.

Sam's fingers moved up to Bianca's neck, and Bianca's fingers moved with them.

This was how she'd done it. Sam had killed Peter after all.

"Peter," Bianca whispered, and for a second it seemed that she could see him. He was floating in the air, just outside the window, his wry, comedic face staring in at them and wearing an expression of horror.

"What?" said Sam, her grip slackening. She spared a glance over her shoulder before tightening her fingers again.

Bianca looked at Sam, who was no longer her daughter, and saw that everything she'd lived for had been in vain.

"THAT'S IT!" MADELINE cried. She was barely keeping it together as the tires of Jimmy's car screeched up the icy driveway. Bianca's car was already parked and the lights inside the house were on. The car had barely come to a stop before Madeline leaped out of it, leaving Sam the kitten behind in the seat.

Inside, Madeline raced through the house, calling for

Bianca. She heard a muffled struggle from the hall and so she moved in that direction, not seeing the rooms around her. The ghost had its hands around Bianca's throat. It was throttling her. Bianca's arms flopped uselessly at her sides, the strength stolen from them. Madeline raced toward the figures and tried to force herself between the two, grabbing for the hands clasped around Bianca's neck. Bianca's eyes were bulging, her lips going blue around the edges. Her breathing was labored. Madeline could see how the ghost's thumbs were pressed hard against Bianca's windpipe, cutting off her air supply. Bianca's tongue emerged from between her lips and her eyes seemed to be focused on something in the distance. She had seconds left.

"Get off her!" screamed Madeline, shoving the ghost with her shoulder, struggling to shake it off.

The ghost was like a pillar of granite as it tightened its grip around Bianca's throat.

From out of nowhere there was a deep, predatory growl, and the kitten—the real Sam— launched herself from Jimmy's arms at the ghost, digging her claws in as she scrambled up the ghost's leg, up its waist to its shoulder, and then spread out over the ghost's face. The kitten yowled as she dug her claws into the ghost's eyes, and the ghost howled and stumbled backward in pain, losing its grip on Bianca's throat as it reached up to tear the kitten away. Jimmy arrived, grabbing the ghost's arms and wrenching them behind its back while the kitten clung viciously to the face that had once been its own.

Bianca crumpled limply on the floor, her breathing ragged and hoarse. One of her hands flailed at her throat.

"Get me something to tie her up!" called Jimmy, shouting in order to be heard over an unremitting howl that had begun to issue from the ghost's throat. Madeline snatched a scarf from the floor that must have belonged to Bianca, and unwound the one from her own neck, delivering both to Jimmy. He looped one around the ghost's wrists and tied them together, then did the same with its legs. By the time this was finished, all three of them were breathing heavily. The ghost's howl had faded to a low moan. Blood trickled down its face and one eye refused to open, the other was red and bloody at the inner corner.

"What now?" asked Jimmy.

"I don't know," said Madeline, panting and looking around. "Where's Sam?"

"There," Jimmy pointed, and Madeline saw the kitten was now in front of Bianca, sniffing her nose and rubbing her whiskers against her mother's cheeks, marking her with her scent glands. The sight of it made Madeline's throat tighten. She turned away, focusing on the ghost again. How had it gotten here? When had it happened? *Why* had it happened?

Somehow, writing about the ghost had summoned it. Or, maybe the story had just made visible something that was there all along. Regardless, the ghost was here and she would have to deal with it.

The ghost stared at Madeline with its one good eye. "I know you," it said at last.

"You do?" asked Madeline.

"I liked you," said the ghost. "When you came to the hospital. You were sweet."

"Yeah, you can go fuck yourself."

The ghost sneered. "Such language from a morsel. It makes me want to taste you even more."

Madeline glared at the ghost that inhabited the body of the woman she'd loved. The ghost had gotten more articulate. It was getting used to its new life. Madeline wanted to kill it, she realized, the urge intensifying the longer she looked at it. She wanted to grab it by the throat and squeeze the remaining life out of it and watch it die. The desire to do this was as strong as the lust she'd once felt for Sam.

"I know that look," said the ghost, sneering even more. "You're hungry, too."

Madeline laughed and the sound was bitter. "Hungry? Is that what you call it, then—this feeling? This...?" She looked down at her hands. They were shaking.

"That's it," encouraged the ghost. "Just give in to that feeling. Let it consume you."

One bloodshot hazel eye focused on Madeline, watching her like a lion watches its prey—waiting.

"You're here because of me," Madeline said, not caring if Jimmy overheard or what he thought. "I'm the one who did this. I don't know how, but I did."

The ghost was watching her, waiting for her to finish. It didn't seem to care whether or not she gave a reason, but Madeline did.

"I wanted to hurt Sam," she found herself whispering, and as she said it she understood why she'd been writing about a hungry ghost. "I wanted to hurt her because she was hurting herself, which hurt *me*, too, but she didn't seem to care. So I guess, in a way, what I wanted was to control her. To possess her. For what I thought was her own good, but it wasn't. What she really needed was to be free."

Now that Madeline could see the ghost for what it was—a sad, empty thing—it no longer frightened her.

"Why did you become a hungry ghost?" Madeline asked. "You must have had a life before this one, didn't you? I know hungry ghosts live a long time, but they don't live forever. At some point, you were born. Before that, what were you? Who were you?"

The ghost stared at Madeline, its one eye unblinking, and Madeline stared back, unafraid. It's eye flashed, and Madeline saw something, an image reflected as the ghost saw exactly who it had been before.

It remembered, and that memory broke something in the ghost. Eyes rolling back into its head, it opened its mouth and loosed a long and mournful wail, the remaining good eye going dark as the hungry ghost faded away, leaving Sam's dead body to slump uselessly to the floor.

Everything was over in an instant. The end had

happened before Madeline had time to second-guess, before she had time to think or stop it or go for the cat and try to put things back where she thought they belonged, where she had wanted them to be.

"What happened?" asked Jimmy, looking down at Madeline.

She stood up carefully, holding her breath. "It's gone."

"What? The ghost? Is that was it was then?"

"Yes, I think so. Whatever it was, it's gone now. It left this life. I don't know where it is now, but it won't bother us again."

"But what about Sam?"

"She's all right," said Madeline, looking at the kitten where she was curled up against Bianca, nuzzled in the crook of her arm. Both of them were asleep, holding on to each other, unconscious of who the other truly was. "She's with her mom."

PETER WATCHED AS Sam's body crumbled to the floor. He knew it wasn't really her, that she had been gone for so long already, but he lunged forward anyway.

"Sam!" he cried, and Sam's single, once-beautiful eye stared up at him blankly, as unseeing as his own. He half-listened to Madeline as she explained what had happened, how the ghost had left, and how Sam was gone.

"She's with her mom," Madeline was saying, and Peter turned his attention to Bianca, whose body was limp, but showed the signs of steady breathing. The kitten that Madeline and Jimmy had brought with them was curled up in Bianca's arm.

"Wait a second," said Peter, leaving the body behind and crossing the room to examine the kitten more closely. "Do you mean to say that this kitten is actually Sam?"

He peered at the cat, which was snoozing dreamily. In her sleep, her nose twitched, and a little shiver ran through her body.

Peter reached out tentatively, one ghostly hand hovering against her fur.

"Sammy?" he whispered. The kitten's whiskers twitched. Her hind leg kicked. Her nose twitched again. "Sam?" he tried, more insistent this time.

"Sam!" he shouted, and he fought the urge to shake her, but then Peter remembered he couldn't shake a thing, not even a planchette on a Ouija board.

Laughter bubbled in Peter's chest. "Would you take a look at us, Sammy? I'm a ghost and you're a cat. Maybe now we can finally forgive each other."

Sam, or the cat, if the cat was really Sam at all, opened its eyes and yawned. She began licking her front paw, moving the long pink muscle between each of toes, and Peter fought his rising anger as images of their past flashed through his mind. Sam in her underwear, storming out of bed; Sam in a slinky dress, pulling him in; Sam with her bedroom eyes, with her sunshine eyes, with her fairytale gaze speaking wordlessly of what should have been their happily ever after. And then he saw the small orange kitten, cleaning its left paw, rubbing it over its nose and eyes and then settling back into Bianca's arm.

An almost-sob ran through him, but he reached out, placing his hand against the kitten's side. She couldn't feel his touch, and all he could feel was the vague resistance of some physical form, but he could imagine the way her fur must feel, soft, beneath his fingers. Peter couldn't turn back time or return things to the way they were, but at least he could say goodbye.

At long last, he could let Sam go.

CHAPTER THIRTY-TWO

SAM AND PETER's bodies were buried in separate locations in the same graveyard and Bianca attended both funerals, which were held on the same day. Madeline was there, too, sitting quietly a few rows back from the front, next to the man that had been there when Bianca regained consciousness in the lake house.

The autopsies revealed that Peter had died of strangulation and Sam had gone into cardiac arrest. The last memory Bianca had of her daughter had been looking into Sam's eyes while Sam's cold fingers dug into her throat and everything went dark. But no, Sam hadn't been Sam anymore by then.

Because of that, Bianca's last real memory of her beloved daughter had happened much earlier, and under much happier circumstances. It was the memory Bianca clung to as she watched her daughter's body be lowered into the earth.

The weekend before Sam had gotten into the accident, she'd spent Saturday with her parents. The weather had been pleasant and they'd had a barbecue, and afterward, Sam and her mother had gone shopping together. Sam preferred consignment stores, but Bianca had insisted they go to the mall. She wanted to get her daughter something nice. She never got to spoil her anymore. They'd wandered through shop after shop, looking at overpriced handbags and jewelry, Bianca trying at every turn to get Sam excited about something.

"This would look darling on you," Bianca told Sam at one point, holding up a form-fitting dress that cinched at the waist. Sam smiled and shook her head, moving away to the jewelry counter while Bianca rifled through other dresses, searching for something her daughter would like. Finally, she had to admit that there was nothing. Sam would continue wearing shapeless frocks she found for five dollars even if they did nothing to flatter her figure. Bianca had taken this to mean her daughter was hiding from something—someone—although perhaps it had only been herself.

When Bianca had looked up she'd seen Sam holding a pair of earrings—miniature chandeliers that dangled with sparkling blue beads. "Gorgeous!" Bianca had declared, nodding appreciatively as Sam held them out to her.

"These are perfect for you," her daughter had teased.

"Oh, no, please," Bianca had protested, but when she'd looked at her reflection in the mirror she'd seen that Sam had been right, as usual.

"I already paid for them."

Bianca had protested, but Sam had laughed her off and she'd had no choice but to accept the gift.

When she drove Sam home that day, Bianca had considered her mission a failure. Looking back on it now, however, she saw it differently. Maybe what Sam had wanted most of all was to give. Maybe by accepting Sam's gift, she'd given her something after all.

Bianca watched through her tears as dirt was shoveled on top of Sam's wooden coffin. On the other side of the grave, she saw Madeline and the tall, broad man conversing. The man nodded and disappeared, heading out of the graveyard and down the road, but Madeline stayed where she was, shifting uneasily from foot to foot until he returned with a covered carrier, the kind used to transport a pet. By that time, everyone had dispersed save for a few lingering people.

Bianca tried not to stare, but she couldn't help it. She barely knew the girl, and yet the girl had saved her life. She'd never even thought to ask how Madeline had known to go to the lake house, or why she'd been there at all. A moment later Madeline and the man approached her. Small, insistent meows were coming from the carrier. Bianca wiped the tears from her eyes and tried to be polite.

"Thank you so much for coming," she said to Madeline, extending a hand. Madeline took it and they shook awkwardly. "I'm sure Sam would appreciate it."

"You're welcome." Madeline looked to the man at her side and the carrier in his hand. "This is my friend Jimmy, and well…"

"I believe we've met before," said Jimmy, taking Bianca's hand and holding it. His grip was warm and firm and comforting, and something about him put Bianca at ease immediately. "My sincere condolences."

"Thank you," said Bianca, fresh tears springing into her eyes.

"I know this may seem unusual, " Jimmy said, removing the cover from the carrier to reveal a small orange kitten with a white star on its forehead, "but I have this little kitten here, and I think she might like to go home with you."

"Oh," Bianca gasped, staring at the kitten. She had the oddest feeling that she recognized the cat from somewhere, like she'd seen it before. Of course, it had been there during that night at the lake house, hadn't it? But it seemed like she remembered it from somewhere else, somewhere earlier.

"No pressure," said Jimmy, seeming to sense her confusion. The kitten was less understanding. It wrapped its claws through the bars and looked up, meowing insistently, and Bianca did her best to ignore it. It was too soon for her to let anything new into her heart. It would be a long time before she was ready for that, if she were ever ready at all. Jimmy spoke again. "I wanted to introduce you, just in case you were interested. She'll be at my shop in Harvard Square, and you can visit anytime, whether or not you want to adopt her. Let me give you my card."

Jimmy dug in his pocket and Madeline took the carrier from him so he could use both hands. He pulled out a leather wallet and a moment later extracted a thick rectangle of paper that he handed to Bianca. In simple font, it read *Jimmy's Used Cat Emporium*, followed by an address, hours, and a telephone number.

"Thank you," said Bianca, holding the card in front of her.

Jimmy glanced at Madeline and took the carrier back from her, replacing the cover.

"Maybe I'll stop by sometime," Bianca said. She had meant it to be an empty promise, but something inside her told her she would go, and soon.

Jimmy tipped his head and turned to leave. Madeline started to turn away too, but hesitated, looking back over her shoulder at Bianca, her mouth open as if to say something, but then she shook her head and smiled—a sad, regretful smile—and lifted one hand in farewell.

Bianca watched the pair walk away down the cobblestone path to the street, and she stood alone next to Sam's grave until the graveyard was empty. The rows of headstones cast long shadows as the daylight faded, and the dirt freshly mounded over the place her daughter rested looked soft. Bianca knelt at the graveside and placed her hands in the soil, inhaling the sweet smell of the earth.

"I love you," she whispered, "to the moon and back."

Bianca held still as the world turned, cradling all its creatures. Night would fall and day would dawn and the world would keep on turning. Tomorrow, Bianca would go to *Jimmy's Used Cat Emporium* and see about that kitten. Maybe she would adopt it after all.

ACKNOWLEDGMENTS

This book would not exist if not for the following people, to whom I would like to extend my immense gratitude:

Lindy Ryan, owner of Black Spot Books and publisher extraordinaire, thank you so much for everything you've invested in this project. Your help has been truly invaluable;

Toni Miller, my developmental editor, your careful reading and editing was essential in helping this project take shape;

Spring Lee, my faithful reader, tithout your eyes, your attention, and your thoughts, this book would not exist.

Thank you to my writing teachers at Bennington: Shannon Cain, Brian Morton, Askold Melnyczuk, Paul Yoon, and Bret Anthony Johnston.

Thank you, also, to the many teachers and friends who have supported my writing in one way or another over the years: Mrs. Forsyth, Mr. Helvey, Mr. Witten, Gail Newman, Christopher Bolton, Eleanor Goodman, Elizabeth Campbell, Jeremy Bellay, Reyna Clancy, Ben Rudick, Leigh Bennett, and Haydn Cherie.

Mom and Dad: Thank you for trusting me to follow my own path and find my own way. Thank you for life, for childhood, and for inspiration.

And, finally, thank you to my life partner, JJ. The best decision I ever made was to link my destiny with yours. Thank you for all of it.

May all beings be happy.

ABOUT THE AUTHOR

Dalena Storm earned her BA in Asian Studies from Williams College and her MFA from the Bennington Writing Seminars, where she studied fiction but also played in the territory between genres. She enjoys eating, sleeping, sex, and words. She'll read the tarot for you if you're pure of heart.